Copyright © 2025 Verlorene Stift

All rights reserved

ISBN: 9798299037890

Deadly Desire

by

Verlorene Stift

Prologue

Vaughn Aksel moved with the calm precision of a surgeon, not a butcher. Every movement measured, every angle rehearsed. The blade in his hand caught the thin light, throwing a silver crescent across the floor. He didn't rush.

He never rushed. This was art, not slaughter. When the final breath rattled out, Vaughn stepped back to admire his work. Symmetry, silence, stillness.

Another scene, another masterpiece. And as always, he whispered in Norwegian — words only the dead would ever hear. *"Perfection lives only in silence."*

He left before dawn, disappearing into the narrow streets of Ansbach, a ghost in a long coat, boots leaving no sound against the cobblestones.

Chapter One

The bell above Carol West's flower shop chimed as she arranged a fresh row of lilies in the window. Morning sunlight spilt through the glass, golden and warm, washing away the last shadows of her sleep.

Outside, the town hummed with gossip. "Another one last night," a man muttered to his wife as they passed. "Same time, same pattern," the woman whispered back, eyes wide.

Carol paused, her hand resting on the vase. "Another murder?" Too close this time. A shiver slipped down her spine, but she forced it away with a smile as her first customer of the day stepped inside. The flowers smelt sweet and safe.

Chapter Two

The shop smelled of roses and wet earth. Carol leaned over the counter, sketching lazily in her notebook between customers — curls of vines, petals, faces that only half-formed. The shop was small, but it was hers. Her escape.

"Miss West?"

She looked up to see Frau Klein, the baker's wife, clutching a newspaper. Her hands trembled as she slid it across the counter. The headline screamed in bold black letters:

ANOTHER BODY FOUND – SAME PATTERN

Carol forced a sympathetic smile as she wrapped the lilies.

"Terrible business," she murmured.

"Terrible," Frau Klein whispered back, leaning closer. "They say it's always the same time. Same marks. Someone is hunting out there, Miss West."

Carol's smile didn't falter, but something cold flickered in her chest. She'd heard this story before, in another life. She pushed the thought away, sliding the bouquet across the counter. When the door shut behind Frau Klein, Carol touched the small scar just below her cheekbone. Old habits whispered in her blood — the kind of instincts she buried when she chose flowers over fire.

The bell rang again. A man entered, tall, broad-shouldered, his face shadowed under a hood. He asked nothing, bought nothing, only just stood near the orchids for too long before leaving. Carol exhaled, steadying herself. Just a customer, she told herself. Just a man.

But outside, murder whispered otherwise.

Chapter Three

Detective Elias Hartmann hated mornings in Ansbach. Not because of the town—the town was perfect. Too perfect. Clean streets, tidy window boxes spilling with geraniums, old churches standing as if war had never touched them. Ansbach was the kind of place where nothing bad ever happened.

Until now…

He stood at the edge of the alley, a cigarette burning low between his fingers. The body had been removed an hour ago, but the whispers remained. Residents gathered near the crime scene, muttering in hushed Bavarian tones, crossing themselves as if ritual could keep evil away.

Detective Anja Schneider crouched by the chalk outline, her gloved hand tracing the marks left in blood on the cobblestones. Her blond hair was tied tight, her movements precise and controlled. s"Same cuts," she said softly. "Same time of night. Whoever this is… they are not improvising."

Hartmann exhaled smoke into the cold morning air. "Serial killers don't belong in Ansbach. This is a place for pensioners and picnics. Nobody locks their doors here."

"Maybe they should," Anja replied, standing to meet his gaze. "Because he's not finished."

They walked toward the Rezat river. The water flowed calmly and glassy under the pale sun. An old merchant barge sat moored at the quay, polished and kept like a relic from gentler centuries. Children pressed their noses to the rails, listening to a guide explain how the vessel once carried salt and wine.

The scene was safe, harmless, almost storybook-like. And yet, last night, blood had run into these same waters. The church bells tolled in the distance. The sound was pure, eternal, safe.

But to Hartmann, it felt like a countdown.

Chapter Four

Vaughn Aksel leaned against the stone balustrade overlooking the Rezat as the morning crowd drifted past. To them, he was just another traveller, another shadow among the tidy Bavarian streets. But his eyes—cold, unblinking steel—missed nothing.

Across the square, a flower shop spilled colour into the gray town. Lilies, roses, bundles of green. It was too bright, too neat for a place where blood had touched the cobbles.

Yet there was something in the arrangement that held his gaze. Stems trimmed to exact lengths, ribbons drawn tight in twin lines, exact and unbroken. No decoration. Just discipline.

Vaughn tilted his head. Most shops cluttered their windows with noise, hoping beauty came from abundance. This one obeyed a sharper rule. Symmetry. Silence.

His thumb brushed the scar across his lip. He knew order when he saw it. This was not chance, it was discipline. Whoever worked inside had a hand that understood lines the way he did.

He watched the flowers a moment longer, not for their colour, but for the geometry that calmed him more than prayer. He whispered in Norwegian, low enough for the river to keep: "Soon." The church bells tolled noon, and Vaughn slipped into the crowd, unseen—but not gone.

Chapter Five

Detective Elias Hartmann dropped a folder onto the table with a dull thud. Photographs spilled across the surface—faces of the dead, eyes forever frozen. Anja Schneider pulled them into a neat line, her brow furrowing deeper with every glance.

"Look at this," she said. "First victim: Turkish woman, mid-thirties. Second: German man, twenty-five. Third: a Black student from Cameroon. Fourth: Polish nurse, fifty years old. Two women, two men. Different races, different ages. Not a specific type, Elias."

Hartmann lit a cigarette despite the no-smoking sign. "Serial killers always have a type. That's how profiling works. This isn't a killer—this is chaos. Random slaughter."

Anja shook her head. "No. It's not random. Look at the precision of the cuts. The timing. Always in that narrow window when the town believes itself safe. This is ritual. He's not killing for rage, or lust.

He's creating something. "But what?" Hartmann exhaled smoke toward the ceiling.

"You're telling me we've got a man who doesn't care if his victim's a man or a woman, Black or white, young or old. He just… chooses?"

"Exactly," Anja said, her voice low. "Which makes him unpredictable. And that makes him impossible to stop."

Through the office window, the town looked postcard-perfect: clean streets, red rooftops, church spires piercing a pale blue sky. On the table, the photographs whispered of chaos.

And somewhere out there, Vaughn Aksel—prepared for another night.

Chapter Six

Rain had polished the cobblestones into a dark mirror. The Rezat murmured beyond the trees, a thin, constant hush like a secret being kept. Vaughn Aksel stood in the mouth of a narrow alley and watched the visitor drift past the shuttered cafés—young, sun-browned,… a holiday smile still clinging from the evening's beer and music.

The man checked his phone, laughed at something on the screen, and looked up to orient himself. Church spire. Streetlamp. It was the sense of a town that promised order, safety, sleep. Ansbach made people careless. That was why Vaughn liked it.

He stepped from the shadow as the visitor reached the blind corner by the old brick wall. A greeting in soft German, harmless as rain. The man turned toward the voice. Vaughn's gloved hand closed, not cruelly but decisively, and the steel whispered once. No struggle. No drama. Just the clean surrender of breath leaving a body that did not yet understand it was gone.

Silence settled. The clock in the square began to count the hour—two distant chimes carried across the water. Vaughn worked without haste. He arranged the man on the bench by the river path, head tilted as if listening to the current, hands folded neatly over the chest.

He brushed a thumb across the lips, leaving the faintest suggestion of a line—as if the face shared Vaughn's own old scar. Not mocking. Marking. He studied the composition: the dark of the coat against the pale stone, the eyes turned toward the river's sheen. Symmetry, stillness. A fragment of order in a world that lied about being safe.

In Norwegian, he breathed to the night—too quiet for anyone living to hear: *"Perfection lives only in silence."*

Then he walked away, boots soundless on the slick stones, and the town returned to its careful sleep.

Chapter Seven

Mist slid off the Rezat like a pale veil, blurring the far bank and the tidy half-timbered houses that watched the water. Detective Elias Hartmann lifted the tape for Anja Schneider as CSU knelt by the bench.

The town still smelled of morning: fresh bread from the Bäckerei, damp stone, a hint of coffee from the café that would open in thirty minutes. Clean. Orderly. As if the night had imagined its own sins.

The victim sat the way the living never would—hands folded, head tilted toward the river as though listening to the current. A young man, mid-twenties, sun-browned, the kind of skin that remembered beaches more than Bavarian springs.

His eyes were open. His mouth almost smiled, except for the fine mark across the upper lip, a suggestion of a scar that wasn't his. "Tourist?" Hartmann asked.

Anja crouched, reading the quiet details of the scene. "Backpacker wristband. Hostel keycard in the pocket. Spanish written on the metro card sleeve. We'll confirm with the hostel."

CSU called measurements in low voices, respectful as in church. A photographer's shutter clicked like a metronome. On the quay, a preserved merchant barge rocked gently against its moorings as a guide set out placards for the first tour of the day. Two early joggers slowed by the tape, whispering in Franconian dialect—"Schon wieder. Gleiche Zeit, oder?"—before moving on with apologetic nods to the officers.

"Same window," Anja said, checking her watch. "The silence's clock."

Hartmann's gaze traced the line of the river, the clean sweep of cobbles rinsed by night rain. "And no struggle."

"Not one we can see," Anja replied. "He either incapacitates them instantly or chooses places where surprise is absolute." Hartmann frowned at the folded hands. "The posing is deliberate. He wants the town to find them tidy."

"He wants us to look," Anja said. "To see composition." She indicated the lip. "And that line again—subtle, almost respectful."

Hartmann grunted. "Respectful? He murders tourists on our river bench."

"Respectful in his own logic," she said, standing. "It's ritual. An idea of beauty."

A uniform approached, cap in his hands. "Herr Kommissar, Frau Kommissarin… the hostel confirmed a missing guest. Javier Morales, twenty-four, checked in yesterday from

Valencia. Friends said he went for a walk after midnight to see the old quarter by moonlight."

Hartmann closed his eyes briefly. The church bells tolled six, bright and harmless. Somewhere a baker laughed; somewhere a child tugged a parent toward the ducks. He opened his eyes to the body, folded like a prayer that had lost its words.

"Release for transport," he said. "Careful with the hands. CSU, I want every fiber off this bench. Every footprint within twenty meters."

Anja lingered a moment longer, absorbing the frame—the barge, the bench, the water like glass. "He escalated placement," she murmured. "Public, picturesque. He wants the town to witness the lie: that nothing bad happens here."

Hartmann looked toward the first customers at the café door, a pair of pensioners offering the officers a quiet "Grüß Gott." He returned it automatically.

"We put out a statement by nine. No panic, but we ask for vigilance. We avoid the word serial." "And when they ask why there's no pattern?" Anja asked.

Hartmann slid the cigarette back into his pocket unlit, a concession to the clean air and the watching town. "We tell them the truth," he said. "He chooses anyone."

The river took the morning light and kept its own counsel. Across the quay, the tour guide welcomed a small group with a cheerful script about trade routes and prosperity.

Anja watched the barge's reflection wobble on the surface and felt the wrongness settle deeper. Somewhere between the bakery and the church bells, between the postcard and the tape, a man had made his choice. And he would make it again.

Chapter Eight

The room was as tidy as a confession. White walls. Bare floorboards, scrubbed until the grain lifted. A single wooden table beneath the window, its surface lined with oilcloth. On it, a leather roll lay open—slots stitched by hand, each tool sleeping in its place. Steel glinted with disciplined thought.

Vaughn rinsed his hands, dried them with a linen towel, then set about the ritual that steadied the hours after work. Scalpel. Bone-handled knife. Thread and fine needles for repairs that were not medical. Cotton wadding. Alcohol. A small brush for seams. Each item was lifted, examined for nicks invisible to ordinary eyes, and returned to its slot.

Ordnung was not comfort. It was oxygen. He sat, rolled up his sleeve, and studied the old map of his body—the pale lines and broken geography. The thin slice across the upper lip. The harsher stroke over his eye. The long, quieter seam along his cheek where anger had once tried to teach him a lesson. He touched none of them. Memory did the touching on its own.

The bells of St. Gumbertus rang the half hour. Outside, a cart rattled over cobbles, the vendor calling the day's bread in a voice meant for neighbours, not for hunters.

The city was clean again. It did that. It washed itself each morning and promised nothing bad would happen here.

On the table's corner lay a small hardcover ledger, its pages squared with a ruler's edge. He opened to last night's line: 02:13 – river bench – silence true. Beneath it, a single pencil stroke, so light it barely existed: a horizontal line, unbroken. He considered adding another note, then closed the book. The ledger was for facts, not for the impulses he did not name.

He drew the leather roll toward him and replaced a dull blade with a fresh one. The click of the tiny screw a sound that belonged to no other life.

When the kit was complete, he bound it with the same knot he always used and set it parallel to the table's edge, a breath's width from the ledger. Parallel lines calmed him. They were promises that the world could still be made straight.

He cleaned the window. It did not need cleaning. He marked the factory stamp on the glass, the perfect square of the courtyard below, the geometry of roofs climbing toward the church spire.

A low breeze slipped through. It carried yeast and coffee and—fainter than either—the ghost of something green and wet. Not the river. Something cut. He looked to the sill. There, caught in the rough of the wood, a sliver of green satin, twin lines folded in memory, left by hands that understood restraint.

He must have brushed it from the street last night without noticing. He lifted it to his nose. Lilies, and the honest dirt of fresh stems. He did not think of a shop. He did not picture a face. He only recognized the line the scent drew through his chest, a fine thread that found a place to hook and hold. He set the ribbon in the ledger like a bookmark and closed the cover, letting the weight of the paper keep the green in place.

He boiled water. The kettle clicked off. He drank without tasting. He stood at the sink and watched the courtyard collect sunlight in neat rectangles. Somewhere below, a child laughed; somewhere farther, a delivery van reversed with a polite alarm, the German sort that asked instead of shouted.

He sharpened a pencil. Wrote a list he did not need: oil, gauze, fresh gloves, a new brush. He underlined none of it. Then, on a clean page, he wrote the only sentence that belonged to him, the one he had learned to say as if it explained anything at all:

Perfeksjon lever bare i stillhet.—Perfection lives only in silence.

He closed the ledger and palmed the ribbon once, letting its edge press a faint green line into his skin.

The town would eat breakfast, read headlines, and decide to be brave by forgetting. He would listen for the hour that belonged to him. And when it came, he would choose again by light, by line, by the way a figure moved through the geometry of a safe city that believed itself beyond his hand.

He did not know what name the ribbon would one day carry. Only that, for the first time in a long while, a thought refused to leave when he told it to go.

Chapter Nine

The square filled quietly, as Ansbach always did—no shouting, just the insolent calm of a town convinced that order would hold. Camera crews set their tripods with polite nods.

Pensioners paused with shopping trolleys. Tourists drifted in with guidebooks still open to Baroque façades and the river walk.

On the Rathaus steps, Detective Elias Hartmann adjusted the microphone, the church clock ticking the seconds above his head.

"Guten Tag," he began. "Early this morning a deceased male was discovered on the river path. We are investigating the death as a homicide. We ask the public to avoid speculation and to refrain from sharing unverified information. Bitte, bleiben Sie aufmerksam."

Hands rose. A local journalist from the *Fränkische Landeszeitung* asked, "Herr Hartmann, residents say the case matches other recent incidents. Same time, same marks. Are we dealing with a Serienmörder?"

Hartmann's jaw tightened almost imperceptibly. "We do not use that term at this time. We are examining links between cases. What we can confirm is a consistent time window between two and three Uhr—and a careful presentation at the scenes. We will increase patrols along the Rezat and the Altstadt after midnight. There is no curfew."

Another hand rose. "Is there a pattern in the victims?"

"No," Hartmann said. "Different genders, different ages, different backgrounds. There is no indication that any group is being targeted."

A foreign correspondent lifted his voice. "Tourist safety?"

"We are in contact with hotels and hostels." Hartmann said. "We ask visitors to avoid walking alone after midnight and to use well-lit routes. If you see anything unusual, call immediately. Keine falsche Scham.—do not hesitate out of embarrassment."

He read the appeal from a notepad: CCTV and dashcam footage from 00:30 to 03:30; any sightings near the preserved merchant barge, the cobbled quays, the bridges; anyone carrying unusual tools or a case large enough to hold them. He finished with a quiet, "Wir schaffen das together."

The phrase drew soft nods. People wanted to agree with him. When the microphones clicked off, the square sighed back into itself —children pointing at pigeons, a tour guide lifting a pennant for the noon group, coffee cups clinking like a metronome of normal life.

Ansbach resumed its whisper that nothing bad ever really happened here.

At the Polizeidirektion, the briefing room smelled faintly of coffee and paper. Anja Schneider pinned a fresh map to the board. Red flags dotted the river like an infection.

"Escalation in placement," she said softly. "The barge. The bench. He wants an audience."

Hartmann folded his arms. "We just told the press there's no pattern."

"Externally, no," Anja said. "Internally: ritual, precision, an aesthetic logic. He kills inside a strict hour, arranges hands, leaves the face marked—subtle line at the lip. He's curating the scene. It's composition."

"We can't arrest a philosophy," Hartmann muttered. "What do we do?"

Anja pointed at the map. "We map lighting gaps and CCTV blind spots within five hundred meters of each site. We canvass hostels and backpacker bars for anyone seen alone after midnight. Ask bakers, delivery drivers, and cleaners with pre-dawn routes for dashcam footage.

Flag purchases of specialist blades surgical steel, custom sharpeners. And we get CSU to reprocess fibers from benches and railings on the quay." He nodded, already assigning teams in his head. "We also run the river. Diver team at dawn if he cleans tools, he may do it there."

Anja added a final note to the board: 02:00–03:00—stricter patrols. Foot, not cars. Quiet, not lights.

Hartmann glanced through the glass at the tidy courtyard beyond—swept, planted, perfect. The world outside did not look like a place where a man could vanish after making death look so neat. He tapped the map. "Tonight we see if order can outwait him."

Anja capped the marker, her reflection faint on the glass between the room and the courtyard. "He's listening for the hour," she said. "So are we."

Chapter Ten

By ten, the square had swallowed the press conference and returned to its familiar softness.

The bell over Carol's door chimed in polite intervals: a pensioner for tulips, a young couple for a thank-you bunch, a mother with a stroller asking for peonies that weren't yet in season. They spoke in whispers, as if volume would tempt misfortune.

"They say the police won't use the word," the mother murmured, adjusting a blanket. "But it's the same hour, always."

The pensioner shook his head. "Ach, Ansbach. Nothing bad happens here. It will pass." He paid in exact coins and wished Carol a quiet day. Quiet felt like an instruction.

Between customers, she wiped pollen from the counter and skimmed the front page of the *Fränkische Landeszeitung*. The headline sat heavy. She closed it and reached for lilies, trimming stems to a clean angle, the scent green and faintly sweet. Her skin tugged faintly; she ignored it.

She had chosen flowers over fire. She would choose them again, every hour if necessary. The phone rang. Not the cheerful jingle of the counter bell but the older landline's clipped tone from the back office.

Carol slipped past buckets and ribbon spools to answer.

"West's Florals, guten Tag."

A man's voice, neutral German, the kind you couldn't place to any region.

"Lilies," he said. "Only lilies. Twelve. No filler. Stems cut to siebenunddreißig Zentimeter. Ribbon—green, bound twice, side by side. No flourish. No bow. Card text: Für die Stille. Pick-up at fourteen. Cash."

The order wrote itself beneath her hand before she realized she was already moving the pencil.

"Name for the ticket?" she asked.

A pause. Not long—exact.

"No name." The line clicked dead.

Carol stood with the receiver in her hand and the pencil pressed to the order book. She listened to the dial tone as if it might confess something. Then she set the handset down and read what she'd written. Specific. Measured. Parallel wraps. No bow. Not illegal. Not strange enough to call the police, but strange enough to itch under her skin.

She trimmed twelve stems to 37cm, laid them in a neat row, like soldiers exhaling, and reached for the ribbon. She looped the satin twice, neat and level, ends hidden. Her hands knew the measure before her thoughts caught up.

When she tightened the second pass, the satin pressed into her skin and left a faint green mark along her ring finger—two lines, side by side. She rubbed them away. They didn't want to go.

A tourist couple came in laughing too loudly for the town's mood and asked for something cheerful for the boat tour. Carol made them a small bouquet of gerberas and mint, tied with white cotton, and smiled as they left. When the door shut, the shop's quiet returned like a held breath released.

She wrote the card slowly: Für die Stille. —For the silence. Her pen hesitated over the final period, as if punctuation could change meaning. She slid the card into its sleeve and tucked it beneath the lily heads where only the recipient would find it.

At thirteen-fifty-eight, the bell chimed. A young man in a courier's jacket stepped in, cap low, mask still a habit from another year.

"Pick-up for two o'clock," he said, eyes flicking to the ticket number she'd taped to the till. He counted out cash—crisp sequential notes, more than the total. "Keep the change," he added with a shrug that felt rehearsed.

He lifted the lilies as if they were instructions and left with the same quiet in which he'd arrived. Carol watched the door close on the neat street and listened to the tiny echo of the bell settle back into the wood.

On the counter, a dusting of orange pollen had fallen in two narrow stripes where the ribbon had rested. Parallel. She brushed them into her palm and they stained like memory.

Chapter Eleven

Vogel slid three envelopes across the table. "First: the lip incision — shallow, precise, made within minutes of death. Controlled to the millimetre." She tapped the next. "Second: residue of diamond polishing compound, three-micron grade. Specialist use — surgical steel, fine tools. Not hardware-store material."

The third: "Two green filaments. Rayon/poly satin ribbon, domestic batch, narrowed to three manufacturers." She held up a transparent sheet. A faint tread had been lifted from the soil.

"Partial outsole: hiking boot, EU 44." Vogel added, "Thumb pressure under the jaw. He closes the airway as he works. Death is fast."

Hartmann straightened. "Danke, Frau Doktor."

Maps and lists bloomed across the squad room cork-boards. Anja drew a tidy column headed: florists for green satin ribbon, trades that used diamond paste, and outdoor shops selling boots in size forty-four.

Hartmann parcelled tasks with the calm of a man setting a table. "Zwei Streifen canvass florists and craft suppliers within city limits. No alarms—ask for unusual orders, large purchases of green satin, or custom cuts. Another team hits watchmakers and jewellers for diamond compound sales.

We request sales logs from wholesalers. CSU keeps combing the riverbank and quay rails for more fibers."

Anja added a final note: CCTV & dashcam cross-reference with shoe size/pattern; look for long coat, leather roll, case. She paused, pen tip resting on the board. "He's tidy. He blends. He moves when the bells are silent."

Hartmann glanced at the clock. "Tonight we walk, not drive. Foot patrol along the Rezat, no blue lights, no heroics."

Outside the window, Ansbach's afternoon went on being beautiful: window boxes bright, a barge tour drifting by to a guide's gentle monologue about trade routes and peace. Inside, the board acquired its first real thread: a ribbon the colour of order, tugging them toward a man who worshipped silence.

Chapter Twelve

No sirens. No radios crackling. Just shoes, breath, and the sound the river makes when the town is asleep.

Hartmann and Anja walked the quay in plain clothes, dark coats turned up against a mild, damp wind. Two other pairs shadowed the bridges upstream and downstream, checking the pools of light where lamps fell short and the places where tree canopies turned cobbles into blind strip of film.

At 01:58, a cyclist whispered past with a bell that barely rang—the little silver note dissolving as if the night refused even that. On the preserved barge, a security chain held the gangplank. A laminated sign flapped once — *Besichtigung* 10–16 Uhr — and lay flat again.

"He likes clean frames," Anja said quietly. "Benches, rails, water. No rubbish bins in shot."

Hartmann nodded. "And he doesn't improvise. He chooses the dead hour before he chooses the person." They paused at a gap between two streetlamps where a plane tree threw a net of shadow across the path. Anja held up her phone—screen dimmed, camera recording.

On playback, the shadows flickered so completely a figure could stand at the rail and vanish between frames. She marked the GPS. "Blind enough."

02:11. Footsteps on stone—measured, not hurried—crossed the bridge upstream, then stilled. Hartmann touched Anja's sleeve, and they faded into the recess of a doorway, letting their silhouettes break against the brick instead of the open air.

A man appeared on the opposite bank, tall in a long coat, hands in pockets. He stopped at the railing, facing the water.

"Tourist?" Anja breathed.

"Maybe," Hartmann said. "Or he knows we'll look and he's giving us a tourist."

The man stood without fidgeting. Not smoking. Not checking a phone. The river wrote light under him, and the streetlamp pencilled a neat line along his profile.

After a minute he turned and walked into a side street where the lamplight ended in a hard edge.

By the time they crossed the footbridge, the street was empty—only a delivery van idling with its hazard lights ticking like a polite metronome. Anja scanned the stone at the corner where the man had paused. Nothing dropped, nothing scuffed. Only the faintest damp print where a sleeve had rested on the rail; it darkened, then disappeared as the breeze changed.

02:51. Hartmann and Anja reached the bench where the tourist had been found at dawn.

02:57. The second patrol checked two students on a bench—false alarm, just beer and a blanket.

"He'll avoid this spot for a while. He hates repetition that looks like laziness."

"He likes repetition that looks like order," Hartmann said. "But not obvious patterns."

They walked on. A fox crossed the path ahead of them, noiseless as thought, and slipped into the shrubbery without breaking a twig. Somewhere a church clock tried out a single chime as if clearing its throat before three. The town slept in good faith.

03:04. A whisper of movement on the upper promenade—coat, shadow… then nothing.

Anja and Hartmann reached the stairs in time to meet a figure coming down:… a baker in a white jacket, flour still ghosting his cuffs, keys in hand for the morning's first batch. He startled at them and then smiled, embarrassed.

"Entschuldigung. Früh."

"Guten Morgen," Hartmann said, standing aside. "Anything unusual?"

The baker frowned, thinking like a man who preferred exact measurements to stories. "Nur… ein Mann stand lange am Geländer. Ohne Handy. Ganz still." He gestured upstream. "Ich habe weggeguckt. Ist unhöflich, jemanden anzustarren."

Anja thanked him, noting the time and location. When they returned to the rail she traced the same place he'd indicated with a gloved fingertip. A line of condensation had formed where a forearm might have warmed the metal. It evaporated as she watched.

At 03:07, the river resumed being just a river. Patrols checked in, quiet and empty-handed. Hartmann looked at the neat town that kept its promises and the water that kept its own.

"He was out," he said.

Anja slid her phone into her pocket with the new GPS mark saved. "And he saw enough to keep liking the view." They walked back without speaking, counting lamps, counting shadows, counting the small places where a man who loved order could step inside it and disappear.

Chapter Thirteen

The sky had the clean grey of a plate waiting to be filled. Carol swept fallen petals from the threshold and flipped the sign to Offen for the last hour.

The square moved at a Sunday pace, though it wasn't Sunday—strollers, soft talk, a violinist practising scales somewhere she couldn't see.

The bell chimed. A man stepped in and paused just inside the door, backlit by the pale street. Coat collar up, cap low, scarf high. Not suspicious—just winter-tidy. The front lights caught glass and threw her reflection back at her; his face sat behind the reflection like a second room she couldn't enter.

"Guten Abend," she said, smoothing her apron. "Kann ich Ihnen helfen?" His voice came in standard German, clear and neutral. "Lilies, Twelve. Stems to siebenunddreißig Zentimeter."

Her fingers recognised the numbers before her mind did. She moved to the buckets, counting quietly as she worked. "Ribbon preference?" He glanced toward the counter where spools sat in tidy rows. "She bound the lilies in mirrored passes, flat and spare, no bow to soften the line." She nodded, throat dry for no reason she could name. "Card?"

"Nein." His hands rested in his coat pockets. Not restless. Not searching. Just present, as if he had practiced the shape of stillness and liked how it fit.

Carol trimmed the stems to thirty-seven centimetres, the measure sliding out of her like breath. She laid the lilies in a straight line and reached for the green satin. Two parallel wraps. No bow. The ribbon slid against her skin and left two faint lines that faded, then didn't. She tucked the ends under themselves, invisible. As if the bouquet were a small problem in geometry, and he was waiting to see if she would solve it cleanly.

"Bar oder Karte?" she asked, setting the finished lilies on the counter.

"Bar."

He placed exact notes—crisp, edges aligned—beneath the till's shadow A glove brushed the counter wood; the leather left no sound. He lifted the bouquet without testing the weight. The lilies looked correct in his hand, as if they had been drawn first and the rest of the scene sketched around them.

"Schönen Abend," she offered.

"Auch Ihnen," he replied, already turning.

The bell chimed once and the door closed on his back. The street returned as if he had simply been weather passing through. Carol stood with her palm on the counter. When she lifted it, a dusting of pollen had fallen in two narrow stripes. Parallel. She brushed them away, and they stained lightly.

Smelled of paper, starch, and the tidy ambition of small commerce. Anja Schneider showed her badge and the fiber photo; the manager adjusted his glasses and led her to a wall of ribbons stacked by shade like a disciplined rainbow.

"Rayon/Poly satin, neun Millimeter, Apfelgrün," he said, pulling down a reel. "Domestic batch. Three shops in the old town take this colour on standing order. We have the last quarter's invoices." He printed them with the pride of a man whose machines behaved.

Back in the car, Anja read the list. West's Florals sat among two others—perfectly ordinary. She circled the trio and wrote: query unusual orders; ask for cash pickups; note specific instructions (parallel wraps/no bows). She checked her watch.

"Tomorrow morning," she said to Hartmann over the phone. "We start with the ribbon."

"Bring coffee," Hartmann answered. "If this is nothing, we'll need it."

Anja looked toward the old town where window boxes still held their winter greens like a promise. The day folded into evening with German punctuality, precise as a timetable. Somewhere, someone was already counting hours again. She underlined West's address and closed the file.

Vaughn carried the lilies along the river where the lamps woke one by one. He did not look in windows. He left no footprints where water could remember them. In his coat pocket, the receipt lay folded to a line as straight as a blade. He did not unfold it. He preferred the weight of the stems to the weight of paper.

He thought of the two green bands tightening under careful fingers, of the way they had held without a knot. He did not think of a face He had not seen one. The bells marked the hour. He measured the sound, then stored it. The town promised itself another quiet night. He promised nothing. The breeze changed.

Chapter Fourteen

The old town opened its eyes the German way—shutters up, pavements washed, a quiet promise that the day would behave. Hartmann and Anja split the list from the wholesaler and began with the smallest of the three ribbon accounts, a shop that sold more greeting cards than stems.

Polite owner. No unusual cash orders. No green satin beyond gift wrap at Christmas. The receipt printer that sang like a toy.

The second florist was brisk, efficient, and offended on principle by the idea of murder intruding on proper work. Yes, they stocked nine-millimetre satin in Apfelgrün. No, they hadn't had any peculiar instructions.

Their orders were online; their customers predictable. The owner offered them coffee and a lecture on wreath trends. Anja smiled, took the list of regulars, and left with clean hands.

Carol had the door propped with a wedge and a broom leaning like a companion. She looked up from trimming tulips when Anja showed the badge. Hartmann stood back a pace,… letting the shop's scent work on him: wet stems, soil, lilies declaring themselves without shouting.

"Frau West," Anja said gently, "we're asking florists about specific ribbon purchases and any unusual orders in the last two days. May we ask a few questions?"

Carol nodded, wiping her hands on an apron that had surrendered to pollen years ago.

"Of course. I keep an order book." She slid a ledger across the counter, its columns straight as rails.

Anja laid the fiber photo down—green satin, rayon/poly weave magnified until it looked like a landscape. "Do you stock this color and grade?" "Apfelgrün, nine millimetre, satin."

Carol reached for a neat stack of reels. "Yes. Domestic batch. We use it for spring work." "Any cash orders with specific instructions?" Anja asked. "Parallel wraps, no bow, precise stem lengths?"

Carol's fingers hesitated for a pause, then she turned pages. "Yesterday. Telephone order at 11:22." She tapped the neat handwriting. "Twelve lilies. Stems at siebenunddreißig Zentimeter. Green ribbon, two parallel wraps, no bow. Card text: *Für die Stille*. Courier pickup at fourteen."

Hartmann glanced at Anja. The phrase sat between them like a coin. "The courier?" Anja prompted.

"Young," Carol said. "Wore a generic jacket. Paid cash—crisp notes. Took the bouquet and left. No chat."

"Any cameras?" Hartmann asked, scanning the ceiling corners.

Carol shook her head. "Only the square's municipal camera." She gestured toward the window. "It sees the doorframe, not faces. Light reflects in the glass."

Anja made a note: Request Rathaus cam, 13:45–14:10. She closed the ledger. "Any other orders like this?"

Carol glanced at the reels, then toward the threshold as if the air there still remembered a shape. "A man came in late afternoon. Ordered the same—twelve lilies, siebenunddreißig Zentimeter, green ribbon, two wraps, no bow. No card that time. He stayed by the door—the light… I couldn't see his face clearly."

"Accent?" Hartmann asked. "Standard German." Carol managed a small smile. "Polite."

Anja's gaze drifted to the work counter. Two faint dustings of orange pollen lay in narrow stripes where a ribbon had rested. Parallel. She didn't touch them. "May our technicians swab for fibers?" "Of course," Carol said. "I'd prefer if the town stopped whispering."

Hartmann took down the order details, the times, the cash amount. He didn't press for a face; there wasn't one to take. "We may return with more questions. Until then, be cautious closing after dark."

"This is Ansbach," Carol said lightly, tying cotton around a bunch of mint. "We do cautious by instinct."

Outside, Anja watched the municipal camera blink its indifferent eye over square. She pictured a figure in the doorway, backlit into anonymity, hands resting in pockets. She wrote: phrase: Für die Stille; parallel wraps; 37 cm; cash; courier; backlit.

"We have a thread," Hartmann said, tucking his notebook away. *"Not a rope. But it pulls."* "He's curating," Anja answered. "And he shops where the composition begins."

Chapter Fifteen

The Rathaus server room was cooler than the offices above, humming with the orderly confidence of machines.

A technician from the Digitalisierungsstelle slid a consent form across to Anja Schneider and tapped the GDPR clause with a pen. She signed; Hartmann initialed.

The technician nodded and queued the feeds: Marktplatz dome cam, arcades, two street approaches, and the small unit facing the florist's door. Timestamp: 13:45–14:10, previous day. On the screen, West's Florals held its reflection like a postcard.

At 13:58 a figure approached: courier jacket, cap low, face was lost to the sunlit glass. He paused precisely where the camera's angle surrendered to glare.

At 14:00 the bell inside must have chimed—his head tipped, he stepped in, and the doorway became a white bar of winter light.

14:04. He reappeared with lilies in hand—stems neat, the green bands winked once in the light—two lines tight as if drawn with a ruler. He moved like a man accustomed to carrying things level. No swing, no bounce. The bouquet never tilted.

"Freeze there," Anja said.

The technician stepped frame by frame. At the lowest edge of the image, the camera found what light missed: boots. Eight-lug forefoot, siped grooves, worn evenly. EU size approximately forty-four, if you trusted the step against the joint in the cobbles.

Hartmann leaned in. "Same pattern as the riverbank."

"Consistent," Anja agreed. "Not proof. But the same grammar."

They followed the courier down the arcade. Another camera picked him up for three seconds, then lost him where a plane tree threw moving lace onto the pavement. Two minutes later a side-street feed found him again, now astride a black cargo bicycle with no logos, the bouquet laid in the shallow front tray like an instrument in its case. He pedaled once and was gone, swallowed by a gap between buildings the city hadn't yet granted a camera.

"Stadtkurier?" Hartmann asked, eyeing the jacket.

The technician zoomed on a stitched patch. Not a logo—just the ghost of one. The cloth had been unpicked. Threads remained like a scar.

A thrift shop near the station smelled of starch and stories. The owner remembered a donation of old courier jackets three weeks back—no names, no receipt, cash purchases all week at two euros apiece.

"People like uniforms," she said apologetically. "They feel useful."

At a small courier cooperative, a manager showed Anja a box of retired patches, the edges singed where they'd been heat-set. "We rebrand every few years," he said. "Jackets go to charity. Bikes sell second-hand."

He pulled a list of recent cargo bike sales: three private buyers, none paid by card. Anja took photos, dates, and the serial numbers that didn't matter.

Back at the screen, the technician pulled a street-level feed one block over and did not hide his small satisfaction when a bicycle bell chimed on the audio track.

The courier passed at 14:07, bouquet steady. A passing delivery van's side panel offered up a reflection—two parallel green bands winking once before the van turned.

The technician froze the frame. "There." Anja wrote: Parallel wraps reflected; cargo bike, unbranded; boots match pattern; jacket with removed patch. She added: route knowledge—blind spots exploited.

Hartmann checked the time on his watch, though the server clocks were more honest. "It's thin," he said. "But the thread holds." "Enough to ask bike shops for a black cargo with front tray sold in the last month," Anja said. "And to canvass thrift shops for courier jackets."

The technician exported the clips to encrypted drives and signed the chain-of-custody form without drama. When they stepped back into the Rathaus corridor, the building smelled like wax and old wood, the kind of cleanliness that collects decades without noise.

Outside, the square made its soft afternoon sounds—cutlery, bicycle bells, a child learning to say Entschuldigung correctly.

Anja tucked the drive into an inner pocket and watched the florist's window hold its reflection like a shield. Somewhere between two cameras and a plane tree, a man had folded himself into the city's blind grammar and ridden away. She underlined the time again: 14:00—routine, ordinary—proof that the ritual didn't only belong to the night.

Chapter Sixteen

Anja Schneider had a list and Bavarian patience. She showed the CCTV stills at three bike shops, all within a ten-minute ride of the square.

Two shook their heads—no black cargo bikes sold recently, no service tags matching the shape on screen. At the third, a mechanic wiped grease from his hands and frowned at the photo like a crossword clue he almost had.

"We serviced a used Bakfiets with a shallow front tray last week," he said. "Cash buyer. Tall, quiet. Didn't try to haggle."

He produced a handwritten receipt with the world's shortest description: Gebraucht – schwarz – Bar. No name, no phone.

"He asked about reflective tape. Wanted none."

Anja noted the date—two days before the lilies order—and the time: late morning.

"Boots?"

The mechanic shrugged. "Work boots. Clean." He shook his head at logos. "Jacket had a shadow here a patch used to be."

Across town, Hartmann visited a watchmaker whose window displayed chronometers so precise they made seconds feel like a moral choice. Inside, the air smelled of oil and restraint.

"Diamond paste, three micron," Hartmann said, laying Vogel's report on the glass. The watchmaker nodded without looking surprised and produced a ledger with neat, square digits.

"We sell to instrument technicians, hobby luthiers, surgeons who sharpen their own," he said. "Last week: five units to a private buyer. Cash." "Description?"

"Tall. Northern accent, not Bavarian. Gloves—thin leather, even indoors. He did not like fingerprints," the watchmaker said mildly.

Hartmann's pen paused. "Accent?"

"Hard to place," the man said. "Not English. Not French. Clean vowels." He tapped the ledger. "He asked if we had smaller grades. He knew what he wanted."

Vogel rang Anja as she crossed the Marktplatz.

"Ribbon fibers from West's counter match the bench blend," she said. "Rayon/poly satin, same domestic batch. No usable prints." Anja stopped under the Rathaus eaves and watched a barge tour group drift along the Rezat.

She wrote on her pad: bike – used Bakfiets, cash, no tape; jacket w/ removed patch; diamond paste – cash buyer, northern accent; ribbon fibers match.

Hartmann joined her with coffee. "Thin," he said. "Thin," she agreed, "but aligned."

She drew two short green lines in the margin—parallel, out of habit—and closed the pad. "Tonight he'll feel the hour again. If he's as orderly as we think, he may also feel like being elsewhere."

Chapter Seventeen

Rothenburg ob der Tauber wore its medieval heart like a polished badge—timbered houses leaning toward cobbles, watchtowers keeping a vigil that centuries had taught them to trust. The Tauber below moved slower than the Rezat, thick with its own stories.

Vaughn Aksel walked without hurry along a stone parapet where the lamplight pooled in soft coins. He had chosen distance. Not running—re-framing. When order risked becoming a map others could read, you drew a different map.

The woman came off a side path from a small hotel, jacket zipped against the chill, keys threaded between her fingers in the city's old superstition. Hotel staff, late shift—fifty perhaps, local, not a type. She was a shape moving through the frame at the hour that belonged to him.

He didn't speak to her. She turned at the sense of someone there and in the turn he stepped close, unremarkable as a shadow joining another. Steel whispered once. The breath left with the same soft astonishment he had heard in every city that told itself it was safe.

He arranged her against the parapet, hands tucked into her coat as if she'd paused to warm them. Head turned toward the valley. A faint line at the mouth, no more than a suggestion—his private signature reduced to a rumour.

He smoothed a stray hair with two fingers, not because it mattered, but because the frame asked for it. He looked at the scene from three angles, stepped back until the tower's geometry tucked the body into a composition only a patient eye would notice, and nodded once.

No ribbon tonight. No bench. No riverbank rail. Just stone, air, and the certainty of an hour kept. In Norwegian, low enough for the stones to keep the confidence, he said it:

"Perfection lives only in silence."

He walked away along the wall, into a darkness built by masons who had never met electricity, and let the ancient town continue believing that after the watchman's call, nothing bad could possibly happen before dawn.

Chapter Eighteen

The news ran without sound, captions marching like obedient soldiers under an image of stone and mist. Rothenburg ob der Tauber—eine Polizeiabsperrung folded neatly along the parapet. A presenter's lips shaped the words kein Zusammenhang bestätigt. No confirmed link.

Vaughn watched the crawl, not the faces. He measured the cuts of the footage, the way the camera framed the wall so the body could no longer be seen. He lifted his coffee and did not drink. In his coat, the ledger's spine pressed lightly against his ribs, the green ribbon marking a page he hadn't meant to mark. Distance had worked; the hour had held. The press, dutiful, offered doubt—good.

He set the cup down precisely on its saucer and touched the ledger's edge through the cloth, thumb finding the faint line of the ribbon beneath. Parallel thoughts, parallel hours. He would let the river patrols walk in orderly circles tonight while he
redrew the frame elsewhere—or closer. He had still not seen a face. He preferred it that way. For now.

Church bells rolled across the square with their usual confidence. The town agreed with itself again. He allowed the agreement to stand. The bell over the door chimed and Frau Klein arrived with a whisper and a headline on her phone.

"Rothenburg," she said, apology tucked into the word. "So near, and still… far."

She placed the phone on the counter. Stone wall, yellow tape—the kind of photo that tried to be respectful and failed by existing at all.

"Different town," Carol said softly, trimming tulips. "Different story." She wanted it to be true. She wanted the river to belong to ducks and barge tours again. She tied cotton around a handful of mint and inhaled its clean insistence. Safe. It smelled like the promise of it.

When the shop emptied, she restocked lilies, counting under her breath. Twelve in the bucket, stems at neat angles. Her gaze slid to the ribbon reels—Apfelgrün waiting in its niche—and away again. Two faint green bands still lived in the skin of her ring finger if she pressed hard enough to remember them.

She laughed at herself under her breath and opened the window a hand's width to let the air argue her out of superstition.

Outside, a child practised Grüß Gott until an adult smiled and said it back properly.

The conference screen split cleanly between Ansbach and Rothenburg. A liaison from the Polizeipräsidium Mittelfranken sat in the middle tile, hair neat, voice calmer than the photos deserved.

Anja presented first: time window between two and three in the morning; arrangement suggesting rest; absence of visible struggle; the shallow incision at the vermilion border of the lip; trace of diamond polishing compound in prior Ansbach cases; outsole pattern approximating EU 44 with eight-lug siped forefoot; the florist ribbon fibers recovered at the river bench and at West's counter.

"Rothenburg scene differs in placement," she said, pointer steady. "Parapet instead of bench, no ribbon transfer recovered so far. Victim profile shifts again—female, local, approximately fifty. To my eye it's the same hand with deliberate variance to disrupt recognition."

Hartmann kept his arms folded. "Or a copycat who reads local news." He didn't believe it, not fully, but procedure prefers its devils named twice. The Rothenburg Kripo chief leaned toward his mic.

"Our CSU will re-examine for micro-residue of diamond paste and attempt a higher-angle outsole capture on the stair approaches. No CCTV on the wall walk, naturally. We'll scrape what we can from hotel cameras along the late shift route."

Anja added: "Request watchmaker and instrument-tech purchase logs for three-micron compound across the district.

Expand courier-jacket and cargo-bike canvass one radius outward. Update foot patrol patterns: not only benches and rails—add vantage parapets, scenic overlooks, places the town photographs itself."

The liaison summarized into neat bullet points and timelines, state police cadence smoothing edges that didn't wish to be smoothed. "No public linkage statement," she concluded. "Advise vigilance without panic. Details such as the lip incision and ribbon remain internal."

When the call cleared, Hartmann looked through the glass at a courtyard that had already forgiven the morning's rain.

"He moved the frame," he said. "But he didn't change his clock."

Anja capped her marker, two short green lines glimmering at the corner of her notes where she'd underlined nothing in particular.

"He's still listening for the hour," she said. "So are we."

Chapter Nineteen

The hour had already done its work. Vaughn Aksel walked back along the Rezat with the quiet of a man who left no echoes. His coat held the night like a secret; the leather roll under his arm weighed almost nothing. The town breathed in squares of lamplight and shadow, confident in its faith that the river would mind its business until morning.

He turned a blind corner where a plane tree stitched darkness over the cobbles—just as a city bicycle whispered into the same gap. A bell chirped, a tire slid, and the rider swore softly before tipping sideways in a graceless, entirely mortal sprawl.

Vaughn stopped. No hurry. No surprise. He had learned that people broke in different directions when gravity won. This one popped up with both hands first—palms out, fingers splayed—as if presenting evidence that she was, in fact, furious.

"Are you kidding me?" she snapped, half German, half English, wholly awake. "You tall wall of coat! Do you not see with those eyes up there?"

He tilted his head. "Entschuldigen Sie." The apology was correct, tidy. It helped nothing.

She dusted off her skirt, inspected a scuffed knee, then jabbed a finger at the height difference.

"No. Absolutely not. I am not arguing with a lamppost. You—bench. Now."

She marched to a riverside bench and climbed onto it, the bicycle bell giving a single indignant kling as if in solidarity. From her new perch she was level with his mouth.

"Better."

He obeyed. Not because she told him to, but because curiosity was a shape that sometimes required compliance to reveal its edges. Up close, the lamplight painted her face cleanly while his remained in the bench's shadow—cap low, scarf high, the habit of anonymity making its own weather.

She planted a fingertip in the centre of his chest. "Rule one: pedestrians have right of way. Rule two: bicycles are not ghosts. Rule three: if you intend to be a brick wall, paint yourself yellow." The poke came again, firmer.

"Do you understand?"

He had not been touched in anger in years. He had not been touched in jest in longer. Something unreasonably human moved under his ribs.

"Ja," he said. The vowel landed softer than his consonants. She squinted, as if listening for an accent she couldn't quite place.

"Good," she said, and—almost dainty—slapped him. Not hard. Not theatrical. More like the punctuation mark at the end of a sentence she was tired of writing. The sound was small and perfect.

For a heartbeat he simply stood there, startled by the fact of it, by the audacity and the accuracy: she had found the exact centre of a man who never let anyone near the edges.

He saw her properly then because the light insisted: tanned skin, the glint of a nose ring, hair to the shoulder with one side shaved neat, a tiny scar near her cheekbone that his eyes mapped without permission.

Her brown eyes, steady and annoyed. The scent came a half-second after the details—lilies and wet earth and the clean green of fresh stems. A florist's signature his ledger had already learned to bookmark.

She still could not see him; the lamp turned his face into a silhouette that refused translation. "Apology accepted," she

declared, though he hadn't offered another. She pointed at the bicycle. "Help me up."

He steadied the frame without touching her hand. She swung a leg over, checked the bell with a prim little ding, and nodded once.

"Try not to loom into people next time, Riese." Giant.—the word was affectionate only by accident.

"Ich werde daran denken," he said—I'll remember that—and stepped back into the shadow, not because he feared being seen, but because the shape of the moment required distance to be complete.

She pushed off, muttering to the night about men who wore the sky like a hat. The bicycle coasted away, steady, the red rear light winking along the railings like a polite metronome. At the corner she glanced back, but the bench held only its own
history again.

Vaughn exhaled slowly. The imprint of her fingertip still warmed his chest through layers that were not supposed to conduct heat. He looked at the bench, then at the river that had agreed to keep secrets before he was born.

In Norwegian, only for himself, he said the sentence he always said—and found that tonight it did not fit as neatly:

Perfection lives only in silence.

The town arranged itself back into order. Somewhere a church tested a single chime and decided it was not yet time to speak. Vaughn adjusted the line of his coat and walked on, aware of a new thread—green, parallel, persistent—drawing itself through the map he had thought was finished.

Chapter Twenty

The bruise on her knee had bloomed into a modest galaxy. Carol propped one foot on a crate behind the counter and dabbed at it with a cold cloth, half-laughing at herself for arguing with gravity and a stranger in the middle of the night.

The bell chimed for a delivery. She signed for buckets of tulips and a box of lilies, her breath fogging faintly in the doorway. The air smelled of clean stone and coffee beginning somewhere. She checked the bicycle: chain fine, bell slightly ajar, giving a crooked ding that sounded apologetic. "Traitor," she told it, and set it right.

When she rolled the lilies to the sink, two green lines pressed into her ring finger again as if memory had learned to stay. She shook out her hand and set the stems to thirty-seven centimetres, then snorted.

"No," she told the measuring tape aloud, and cut them at thirty-five just to prove a point to nobody.

The square outside rehearsed its first Guten Morgen, the kind people use like a handshake. Carol breathed with it until the shop felt ordinary again. Somewhere in the fresh part of her mind, though, a word kept stepping in and out of the light: Riese—giant. She'd meant it as a joke. It kept sounding like a name.

Hartmann and Anja took their coffee to the bench by the plane tree where the blind corner trimmed camera sightlines into lace. CSU had been and gone; a chalk circle marked a faint smear of dried blood the size of a fingernail on a lower cobble. Next to it, a thin crescent of black rubber arced like punctuation.

"Bicycle slip and a knee," Anja said, crouching. "Fresh between two and three." She nodded at the CSU flag. "Female DNA expected."

A street cleaner, broom parked like a companion, pointed with his chin at the plane tree. "Da war Lärm," he offered. "Nicht Schlägerei—Stimmen. Eine Frau hat geschimpft." He smiled despite himself. "Sie nannte ihn 'Riese'. Hat ihn zum Sitzen auf die Bank befohlen. Wie in der Schule."

Hartmann couldn't help the corner of his mouth. "A witness who approves of discipline." He took the statement, then followed the cleaner's gesture to a scuff on the bench slat.

"Bell strike," Anja said, touching nothing. "Angle fits a handlebar swing." She photographed, logged, and drew a small map of the blind wedge between lamps.

"He was out," Hartmann murmured, echoing himself from nights before. "He met someone. And she walked away."

Anja capped her pen. "We ask clinics for walk-ins with minor knee abrasions, time window three to five. We don't force it. If she wanted police, she'd have called." She added to her pad: witness word: Riese; female knee blood; bell arc; location: mapped blind.

Over the river, the barge's guide rehearsed a cheery script about trade routes and watchtowers as if ancient order could be spoken into the present. Anja looked at the bench a moment longer.

"He let the moment live," she said. "That's new."

The safehouse kept its light the way a museum keeps silence. Vaughn set the leather roll on the table and did nothing with it. He touched the place at the center of his chest where a fingertip had landed with comic authority and found that warmth could be a fact hours later.

He opened the ledger to last night's line: Rothenburg – wall – silence true. Beneath it he wrote, smaller: Rezat bench – interruption – contact – subject uninjured – voice: Caribbean lilt under German.

He paused, pencil weightless, and added a single unruled mark—two short parallel dashes. He did not name them. He pictured the geometry of the encounter instead of the face he had refused himself: lamp, bench, plane tree, bicycle arc; a woman ascending to his mouth by way of a public seat in order to correct a stranger in a coat. It should have been absurd. It had felt like math.

He closed the book and breathed once, measured, to test whether the sentence he lived by still fitted where it belonged. It fit around the first hour. It refused to close around the second. He let the refusal stand and cleaned a blade that did not need cleaning.

Across the courtyard, a child practiced Grüß Gott again and again until it sounded like a word meant to be shared. Vaughn listened to the shape of it without deciding whether he liked the sound.

Chapter Twenty-One

Order looked different where hedges did the counting. In the Hofgarten, the gravel paths met at right angles polite enough to bow. Boxwood held its line. The Orangerie's pale façade reflected a sky that had decided to behave.

Vaughn Aksel walked the perimeter as a man measures a room before moving in—pace, angle, light, the places where a camera would prefer to blink. The reflecting pool offered a frame with its own grammar: water as glass, statue as witness, bench as punctuation.

Too close to a pattern he had already used, unless he shifted the geometry. The balustrade under the orange trees presented a quieter line. He stood there, watching the lamps begin to warm, and counted breath against the distance to the gate. Two plain-clothes officers crossed the far path pretending to be a couple arguing about a dog they didn't have. Patrols, then.

Good. Let them walk the river while he taught the garden to keep confidences. He marked a route through shadow, a place where gravel lay packed enough to leave no story for morning. He did not think of a bicycle or a bench by the Rezat. He did not decide whether the word Riese was a joke or a mirror. He counted, and the garden kept the count.

The landline rang with its clipped, old-fashioned patience. Carol wiped her hands on her apron and picked up.

"West's Florals, guten Tag."

Standard German again. Neutral.

"Lilies. Twelve. Stems to siebenunddreißig Zentimeter. Ribbon: the green bands winked once in the light—two lines tight as if drawn with a ruler. Card text: Für den Klang. Pick-up at achtzehn Uhr. Cash."

For the sound—the word set a small bell moving under her ribs.

"Name for the ticket?" she asked. A short pause that recognized itself. "No name."

The line went dead as if it had fulfilled its purpose perfectly.

Carol stared at the receiver until the dial tone gave up. She wrote the order cleanly in the ledger and underlined the card words once. Klang. Sound. The bicycle bell had made exactly one honest kling last night before she set the world to rights from a bench. The coincidence was silly. The coincidence was not silly at all.

She set stems to 37cm without argument this time and tied the green satin parallel, no bow, ends tucked invisible. When she pressed the ribbon flat, two pale lines warmed along her ring finger like habit. She told them, out loud and cheerfully, to mind their own business.

Frau Dr. Vogel's email arrived with the restraint of a lab report that preferred facts to drama: bench smear, human blood, female. No profile—quantity insufficient. Rubber crescent consistent with bicycle bell strike.

Anja logged it, circled the blind corner again on the map, and widened the evening grid.

"Add Hofgarten and Orangerie balustrade," she told Hartmann. "He played river and wall. Next he'll want a place the town photographs itself."

Hartmann nodded. "Foot patrols in pairs. No lights unless necessary. Quiet routes only."

He glanced at the whiteboard where West's Florals now shared space with two other shops and three bike sellers.

"We sit on the square from 17:45. Municipal cam gives us one angle; we take the other."

At six o'clock, two officers in plain clothes watched the florist's door while the Marktplatz dome camera blinked its indifferent eye. A courier jacket appeared on schedule. Cap low. Face where the reflection lived. The lilies emerged minutes later, green bands catching one neat flash as the figure turned. Boot tread: eight-lug, even wear. The bouquet did not tilt.

Anja, watching from across the square with coffee cooling in her hand, felt the small alignment she always trusted: time, angle, movement.

"He likes routine," she said into the mic that wasn't broadcasting. "Daylight rehearsals for midnight." Hartmann followed the courier into a lane and lost him where a plane tree did its lace trick again. "Blind spot," he said without rancor. "Note it, thank it, replace it."

He marked a request for a temporary camera and returned to the square where life had resumed its practised calm.

Carol stood a moment longer than necessary with her hand on the counter where the bouquet had rested, feeling the ghost weight of stems and the memory of parallel green.

Across town, in a garden designed to obey, a tall man measured the distance between a balustrade and a gate and found that the numbers made a shape he liked.

Chapter Twenty-Two

Gravel agreed to be quiet when asked properly. Vaughn Aksel measured the path under the orange trees, finding the portions packed hard by decades of good manners. The reflecting pool held the Orangerie upside-down, a perfect model of obedience. He noted the lamps—warm circles, polite intervals—and the pockets of hedge where a tall man could be less than a fact.

He carried nothing that would have weight in a story: no case, no bag. Inside his coat, a narrow fold of green ribbon pressed a patient line against his palm.

Plainclothes officers moved in pairs. Hartmann walked with a young patrolman who moved like a former athlete trying to remember how to amble. Anja paired with a CSU colleague who counted light like a scientist, pointing out where a camera would one day live.

"Rails, benches, balustrades," Anja said softly. "He chooses frames that photograph well."

Hartmann nodded. "And he steps into them when no one is looking."

Two figures crossed the far path, arguing mildly about a leash they did not carry. Patrol. He let the garden breathe through them and became part of the hedge—not hidden so much as uninteresting. When they turned, their eyes slid across the boxwood the way water ignores a stone it has already learned.

He moved when they moved—counter-rhythm, the music of absence. At the balustrade he placed a small arrangement made from memory: A dozen lilies lashed with twin green strokes of satin, ends hidden, no bow to spoil the symmetry. The card slid under the stems like a quiet thought: Für den Klang. Not a taunt. A study. Sound marked by absence—bells that would ring later, gravel that refused to speak now.

Anja stopped first. Not at the flowers—at the absence of dust on the balustrade, a clean oval as if a hand had smoothed it. Her gaze followed the edge and found the lilies the way one finds a comma in a line that suddenly makes sense.

"He's rehearsing," she said. "Day orders. Night placement." Hartmann's jaw ticked once. "Card?"

She slid it free with a gloved fingertip. Für den Klang. She didn't say it aloud; the word seemed to prefer the inside of the mouth. She logged the weave, the tucked ends, the satin laid so evenly it could have been measured on graph paper.

"CSU," Hartmann said into the mic. "Hofgarten, Orangerie balustrade. Flowers left within the last quarter hour. Quiet approach." "Footprints?" the patrolman asked.

"Packed gravel," Anja answered. "He asked it to keep a secret, and it agreed."

He watched the small knot of plainclothes gather at the balustrade from a shadow where the hedge thickened. One of them handled the card with laboratory hands. Another scanned the hedge line without belief.

He backed away in straight lines, like a man leaving a chessboard without touching any pieces. The bells waited. He did not. The hour belonged to him whether or not he spent it. He let the garden keep its offer and walked out by the south gate, where the path joined the world without announcing it had changed.

CSU bagged the bouquet, lifted a faint trace of green fiber from the stone, and noted precisely nothing from the gravel.

"Same blend as the river bench," Anja said. "Rayon/poly, satin. Domestic batch." She looked past her own reflection in the Orangerie's dark windows. "And the card matches the order at West's. Klang after Stille. Sound after silence."

Hartmann wrote the words in his book and disliked the poetry of it. "He's not just killing in frames," he said. "He's composing."

Across the reflecting pool, a faint breeze wrinkled the upside-down façade into something imperfect and briefly human. Anja watched it settle back to flawless and decided, for once, to let the metaphor keep its secret until morning.

Chapter Twenty-Three

Vogel's update came in her usual order: "Hofgarten — green satin ribbon, domestic batch; common card stock; trace of diamond paste." From Rothenburg: "Same lip incision. Same diamond residue." Anja tapped the margin. "Same grammar. Different sentence."

The Polizeipräsidium drafted a careful statement: no confirmed links for the public, more patrols in parks and gardens, vigilance urged in the silence's hour before dawn.

At noon, a radio voice repeated it softly, as Bavaria prefers: walk in pairs, report without hesitation. The town bent around the advice and went on.

Then Frau Klein arrived with a photograph on her phone—someone had already posted the Hofgarten lilies to a neighbourhood group. The frame was tasteful: balustrade, Orangerie lights, a bouquet placed with the kind of care people usually reserve for joy.

"Yours?" Frau Klein asked, eyebrow kind rather than accusatory. Carol looked at the ribbon. Two green bands, parallel, ends tucked invisible. She could have picked her own hands out of the picture.

"Anyone's," she said lightly, and meant it in both directions.

She tied cotton around mint and set it in a jar by the window. When the shop emptied, she slid the Apfelgrün reel deeper into the shelf, not hiding it so much as asking it to be humble.

The landline rang. She answered with her usual warmth, but it was only a supplier about chrysanthemums. She laughed at herself after and told the lilies they were not allowed to become characters in a story. They ignored her by being perfect.

The ledger lay open to a page that had begun to look like admission. Vaughn wrote with the same economy he used on skin: Hofgarten — arrangement observed — fiber likely recovered.

He closed the book before the empty space below the line had the chance to suggest anything sentimental. He cleaned a blade already clean and watched the steel find itself in the window's reflection.

The words that had always fit—*Perfection lives only in silence*—sat obediently in his mouth and refused, lately, to occupy his chest. He let the refusal remain. It was information.

He allowed himself one remembered image, trimmed of everything but geometry: a woman on a bench correcting a tall stranger, a fingertip placed with absurd precision at the center of his chest, a bicycle bell pronouncing a single syllable of amusement to mark the moment. No face. Enough shape.

He folded a short length of green satin into the ledger as a ruler and left for a walk with empty hands—through streets that believed in themselves, under lamps that kept polite circles, past a florist's window that still held its own reflection like a shield. He did not stop. He did not need to. Not yet.

Chapter Twenty-Four

Anja Schneider read the text twice before showing Hartmann.

Heute Nacht. Der Kreis. Altstadt Nürnberg. Räume: Stille/Klang. Grün ist der Schlüssel. Tonight. The Circle. Altstadt Nürnberg. Rooms: Silence/Sound. Green is the key.

"Informant?" Hartmann asked.

"Old source," Anja said. "Unpredictable. Always right when it's worst." She looked up. "We go as ourselves."

He didn't ask what that meant. They had their private life the way Germans kept their cellars—orderly, discreet, and nobody's business unless the wine was needed.

The doorbell was a bronze circle pressed with intent. Inside, the hallway glowed the color of expensive honey. A woman in a tailored black dress glanced at their digital invitation and tied a double band of green satin lightly around Anja's wrist. Parallel lines. No bow.

"Stille links, Klang rechts," she murmured. Silence left, Sound right.

Masks weren't required, only common. The air smelled of orange peel and wood polished to a whisper. In the Stille room, people spoke in glances. In Klang, a low pulse of music and laughter braided into a civilized murmur. The rules were posted like art: consent explicit, no phones, names unnecessary, no questions that did not want answers.

Hartmann and Anja moved as lovers who trusted each other do—close enough to look committed, loose enough to look curious. It wasn't a performance. It was a language they already spoke.

A demonstration unfolded like a dance: a woman offered her wrists to a man in thin leather gloves. He wrapped a short green satin twice—parallel, no bow—and tucked the ends under. She nodded once. He kissed the inside of her wrist without touching skin with his mouth.

The room watched not for sex, but for symmetry. Anja's breath moved once in her throat. Hartmann's finger tapped his glass: yes, I see it.

A tall man stood near the doorway, cap low even indoors, face half-shadowed by a copper sconce. Not unusual here—but his stillness was. He didn't fidget or browse. He measured. His vowels were northern when he declined a drink, polite and neutral. His boots were plain, dark, evenly worn. The parquet disguised the tread, but Anja filed the thought anyway.

A watchmaker in velvet held court over a tray of tiny mechanical hearts. "Diamond paste," he said to a laughing trio, "is the difference between almost perfect and perfect. Three micron for elegance. One for obsession." He liked hearing himself say it.

Anja laughed on cue and let him show her the scar from a loupe burn on his thumb. When he turned away, she photographed nothing and remembered everything.

In the cloakroom, a courier cooperative sticker, half-peeled, clung to the door. Beneath it, a row of black cargo helmets sat like obedient thoughts. They climbed to a landing that looked down on both rooms. People arranged themselves like sentences. Anja rested her wrist against Hartmann's chest. Green satin made two parallel lines over his heartbeat.

"We can pull at this," she said. "Stille, Klang, green satin, watchmaker's paste, cargo bikes. Our man could belong here or know someone who does."

Hartmann kissed the inside of her wrist the way the gloved man had done—mouth close, not on skin. "We belong here," he said. "That's why we'll see what others won't."

Downstairs, the tall man from the sconce had vanished the way practiced people do—without door or flourish. Anja watched the gap he left as if it were an object. She felt the room's grammar shift and wrote the sentence in her head: He arrives without a name; he leaves without a trace; the club keeps its story intact.

Anja slipped past a staff-only rope while Hartmann distracted a host with a question about the playlist. In the narrow corridor she found a crate of green satin reels—Apfelgrün, nine millimetre—and a box stamped for the same wholesaler she already knew.

Next to it: a rack of unbranded jackets with stitches where patches used to be, and a wall hook with a key fob shaped like a tiny orange—Orangerie humor.

She photographed with her mind, then with the body cam brooch. Evidence would have to be negotiated later. For now, the story existed: a place with two rooms named Silence and Sound, a preference for green satin and anonymity, a habit of removing logos from uniforms, cargo helmets waiting like punctuation.

They left by a side door like any other couple—warm, flushed, not drunk, not hurried. The alley smelled of winter and baking bread from somewhere already morning. A black cargo bike rested under a lamp that chose not to reveal its frame number. Inside, laughter carried—pleasure without malice—and a woman's shush answered it like a smile.

"Unpredictable enough?" Hartmann asked.

"Predictable where it matters," Anja said, lifting her wrist so the green satin caught the lamp.

"Our man speaks this language. He leaves parallel lines and expects the world to call it art."

Hartmann kissed the space just above the ribbon. Gesture, not mouth. "And we're fluent."

On the way back, they paused over the black water splitting the city into reflections. Anja's phone buzzed—Vogel, nocturnal as ever: Rothenburg paste matches. Internal linkage confirmed.

Anja smiled, small and tired. "Sound after silence," she said.

Hartmann's hand found hers where the green made two patient bands. They walked on, knowing the club had given them a grammar—if not yet a name.

Chapter Twenty-Five

The conference room at the Staatsanwaltschaft was bare except for files and coffee. Frau Staatsanwältin Reiter listened without interruption as Anja laid out the chain: green satin fibers (Apfelgrün, nine millimetres), diamond polishing compound (three microns), outsole symmetry, courier jackets with removed patches, cargo helmets, and a private club in Nürnberg with rooms called *Stille and Klang,* where ribbon was a language.

"You don't have a suspect's name," Reiter said.

"We have a grammar," Anja replied. "We need lawful access to the places it's spoken."

Hartmann kept it practical. "We request a narrowly tailored search warrant—storage areas and back-of-house at Der Kreis. Targets: reels of Apfelgrün satin, unbranded jackets with stitch ghosts where patches were unpicked, cargo helmets, sales logs around key dates, and any internal camera archives. Limited seizure only, proportional to the homicide series."

Reiter nodded once. "Verhältnismäßigkeit is our shield. Adult club, consenting members—no fishing expedition. You'll conduct the search off-hours with plainclothes. No disruption of private rooms unless a judge extends it on site. Business premises have different protections, but we treat them with care."

Anja slid a draft affidavit across. Photographs from the service passage—crates of satin, jackets, a card marked Für den Klang—sat beside the CCTV still of the cargo cycle. Reiter read with the speed of habit, made two pencil edits, and said, "I'll put this before the duty judge by two o'clock."

Later, back at Kripo, maps of the Altstadt marked with modest arrows. Entry via staff door with club manager present, a neutral observer from the Ordnungsamt to keep the record clean, CSU kit staged for low-impact collection. Body cams on, mics low, data officer on call.

"No heroics," Hartmann said. "We're inspectors until proven otherwise. If the judge narrows us further, we smile and comply." Anja added contingencies in tidy script: if a tall male with northern vowels is present, no grab without cause; note gait, hands, glove habits; log footwear when shoes are stored; photograph jacket interiors for stitch ghosts.

That afternoon, Reiter's call to club counsel was as cool and precise as case law. "We respect your clients' privacy. Our interest is limited: procurement records and items consistent with a homicide ritual." She paused, listening.

"Yes, rooms are named *Stille and Klang*. No, we are not policing sex."

By evening, the team had rehearsed the tightrope one last time. If the club was clean, they would leave it cleaner. If it held threads, they'd take only what the warrant allowed—and note everything else for the next paper.

Hartmann closed his folder. "We walk in like we belong and leave without a ripple." Anja thought of parallel green lines and the way a creed could become a map.

"And we listen," she said. "For sound after silence."

Chapter Twenty-Six

The landline rang with its clipped patience. Carol tucked a pen behind her ear.

"West's Florals, guten Tag."

The voice was the same neutral German that never seemed to belong to any town.

"Lilies. Twelve. Stems to siebenunddreißig Zentimeter. Ribbon: green, two parallel wraps, no bow. Card text: Für den Atem. Delivery, please."

Her heart did a small, foolish thing.

"Address?"

"Altstadt Nürnberg, side entrance. Ask for Klang. Password: Grün ist der Schlüssel. Cash at handover. Six thirty."

The line clicked dead as if it had been measured to the second. Carol stared at the receiver, then wrote the order in steady letters. She underlined the card once. Atem—breath. Silence, sound, breath. Someone was composing with her ribbon. Or with her hands.

She built the bouquet slowly, devoutly: twelve lilies, clean angles at thirty-seven centimetres, two green bands parallel, ends tucked invisible. She boxed it for the bicycle—padding, straps, a municipal bell that behaved. When she tried the bell, it gave a neat, confident ding as if to say it had learned its lesson.

She looked at the clock. Enough time to change shoes, not enough to change fate. She told herself it was just a delivery for a private party. She told herself Nürnberg was thirty minutes and a different story away. She told herself she would be careful.

Across the square, a plainclothes observer sipped coffee and watched West's doorway the way people watch weather. Anja's note had stuck: add an undercover to evening pickups.

The observer did not interfere. He counted pedals and seconds. Carol wheeled the cargo box to the curb, checked straps, and set off toward the station road. The bouquet rode level, parallel bands hidden from everyone but the person who knew how to look.

The townhouse door accepted the password like a habit. The host in a black dress weighed the bouquet with practiced hands.

"Perfekt," she said softly. "Für den Atem."

She counted out crisp notes—aligned edges, generous change—and tucked the card beneath the stems.

"May I… see where it goes?" Carol asked before her good sense caught her tongue.

"Another night," the host said kindly. "Tonight, just the handover."

The door closed with a hush that suggested good carpentry and better secrets. Carol stood for one breath longer than necessary, then turned her bicycle back toward the station, telling herself she felt lighter only because the box was empty.

Chapter Twenty-Seven

The S-Bahn hummed with the civilized tiredness Germany wears like a cardigan. Carol sat with the cargo box folded, hands wrapped around a paper cup that smelled more of warmth than coffee. Stations announced themselves in tidy tones.

Nürnberg blurred into Fürth, Fürth into a line of smaller stops that promised nothing except themselves. She checked the bouquet receipt once—crisp, aligned edges—and slid it into her pocket as if paper could remember a heartbeat.

By the time Ansbach welcomed her with lamps and bakery sugar cooling in the air, she wheeled her bicycle past the taxi rank and into streets that belonged to her by habit.

A radio tried waltzes at a sensible volume. At the corner by the plane tree she stopped for a car that didn't need her to stop, laughed at her own courtesy, and pushed off. The bell gave a single, cheerful ding as if it had forgiven the night before.

Vaughn Aksel had taken an earlier train, two carriages away, letting reflections behave for him. Now he matched the rhythm of the streets the way a thought matches breath—present without needing to be noticed.

He walked the long side of the block, not fast, not slow, fitting himself to the lamplight's habits and the places where trees stitched their shadows into lace. He collected only what he needed: angle, timing, the sound of her bell, the way she balanced at a stop she did not owe the car. A lesson in kindness. A map of trust.

At the corner, the bicycle's front wheel kissed a shallow rut. Her balance tipped. A tall figure stepped into the slipstream of motion with the precision of someone who makes frames for a living.

"Nicht erschrecken," he said softly. Don't be startled.

A gloved hand steadied the handlebar, another touched the small of her back before gravity could take its vote. For a heartbeat she thought—helpful. The next, she understood—held.

Her protest was sensible, not dramatic. Her protest was practical, not loud. His palm erased it. The world narrowed to lamplight on cobble, breath against scarf, the exact place where a jaw can be guided so words become air.

She fought in the way practical people do: twist, weight, heel. He absorbed motion without violence, turned it into stillness, kept her upright, kept the bicycle from clattering, kept the moment neat. Of course he did.

"Keine Angst," he murmured. No fear.

Absurd, almost funny—she would have laughed if the night had belonged to her mouth. Something cool circled her wrists—no sting, no snap, just parallel pressure, not pain.

She tried to see his face. The lamp refused. She smelled orange peel and lilies and clean steel that wasn't there and knew, with a small incredulous clarity, that the bench had been a prelude she had somehow written.

"Riese," she breathed into his palm, the word shaping itself out of air more than sound.

He shifted, acknowledging without comfort, without threat. Then the wedge of shadow became a doorway, and the two of them folded into it.

When the street resumed itself, there was nothing to mark the absence but the lace of a plane tree and, on the cobbles, a single green thread so fine it could have been a trick of light.

Chapter Twenty-Nine

Light arrived first—clean, winter-pale, the kind that clarified instead of warming. Carol fixed her eyes on the ceiling trim and counted breaths until the tilt stopped. Citrus and metal lingered in the air. A kettle clicked off somewhere like a period placed exactly where it should.

Her wrists were bound in linen. Not cruel, not careless—parallel pressure, the kind of knot chosen by someone who loved straight lines. She tested carefully. Enough give to feel the edges; not enough to lie to herself. No gag. No blindfold. A kindness that doubled as warning.

She catalogued. Window: a square set high, showing a courtyard arranged into neat rectangles of light. Table: bare wood under oilcloth, a leather roll tied with deliberate spacing from a small ledger. On the sill: a short length of green satin folded once, like a thought saved for later. When she flexed, two faint marks pressed into her ring finger—green ghosts that had followed her from the shop into this room.

She breathed through the panic that wanted rehearsal and let irritation go first instead. "If you kept my bicycle bell as a trophy," she said to the ceiling, "I'll send you the world's most passive-aggressive thank-you card."

A voice answered from where the window refused to light his face. Neutral German, vowels clean, gravity set to calm.

"I don't collect bells. They insist on speaking."

He stepped closer. Tall. Coat removed. Sleeves rolled once, with the same economy he gave to everything. He set a glass of water on the table—near, not yet hers.

"You are not in immediate danger," he said. "You may speak. You will not shout. The neighbours trust these walls. I won't teach them otherwise."

Carol turned her head, meeting the fact of him: the silhouette that had refused translation on the street now translated into posture, into the straightness of shoulders trained to move without apology.

"Rule one," she said. "You give back my bicycle."

"Rule one," he returned without irony, "you keep breathing. The bicycle is in the courtyard. It has forgiven you."

She let out a breath she hadn't meant to hold and hated that he noticed. "Rule two," she said. "You use your words. Men who loom should be required."

"I am using them," he said mildly, and slid the glass closer. "Drink."

She lifted her bound hands as far as they reached. He considered the geometry, then tipped the glass to her mouth with steadiness that made it feel like compromise instead of care. Cold, clean water. She drank because thirst wasn't a hill worth dying on.

"Why me?" she asked, not pleading—curious, the way a florist asks why lilies when the occasion says tulips.

He let the silence weigh itself. "Because you corrected a stranger from a public bench," he said. "Because you needed a better angle to argue and didn't apologize."

"You almost ran me over."

"I almost didn't." He studied her. "The difference interests me."

Her gaze slipped to the leather roll. The words escaped before she censored them.

"Use the one to the far left. It cuts with precision."

He untied the roll and unscrolled steel like a map. Light played across edges as his fingers touched each piece in turn, the way a pianist identifies keys before playing. At last he selected the far-left blade and stepped just far enough into light for steel to speak, not the face behind it.

Carol held still. The linen remembered the knot's logic. But he didn't lift her wrists. Instead he reached for the ribbon on the sill, folded once, and laid it on the oilcloth. The blade descended in a clean, quiet stroke. The ribbon parted. He placed both halves parallel.

"Precision is a tool," he said. "Composition is the work." The blade returned to its slot, far from wrists.

"We will have rules," he continued, as if writing in a ledger. "You may ask for water, for the bathroom, for light or less light. You may ask questions. I may not answer. You will not lie. I will not shout. If you run, I will not be messy."

Her mouth curved, annoyance doing the work fear refused. "Rule whatever-number-we're-on: if you intend to touch me with anything sharp, you warn me first."

He inclined his head, as if she'd improved the draft. "Agreed."

"Good. Then we can discuss your decorating. The parallel lines are getting on my nerves."

Silence shifted in the room. Not threat—attention. He stepped back into the window's square, watching her with a kind of regard that wasn't ownership but might mistake itself for it without correction.

"Tell me your name," she said. "I can't keep calling you Riese. It's rude."

He didn't answer. Names spoil good stories. Instead he said, almost to himself, "Names confuse things." A pause. "Later."

"Later is a name," she countered. "It just pretends not to be."

From the courtyard came a child's Grüß Gott, practiced until it belonged to everyone. The room pared it down to shape.

He lifted the glass again. "More water?"

"Yes," she said, then added, because she refused to surrender her personality: "And when you put the ribbon away, don't stack the halves. Leave them parallel. It'l make you feel better."

He looked at the lines and—almost—smiled. "It does," he said.

He left them parallel. She watched the blade rest far away, the roll closed with care. He watched a woman in linen who refused to be anyone but herself. Between them, rules began to sound like a conversation neither had planned to start.

Chapter Thirty

By half past seven, the undercover across from West's Florals knew the rhythm by heart. Carol usually rolled the shutter at seven-thirty, set two buckets on the step, and propped the door with a wedge. Today, the shutter stayed down, the lights off, the bicycle rack empty. He texted Anja one line: *Shop still dark. No movement.*

By eight, Hartmann and Anja stood outside. The square smelled of bread and wet stone. Hartmann tapped the shutter with a knuckle; it answered with honest metal. No sign in the window—no bin gleich zurück, no delivery note. Anja tried the bell anyway. Nothing. She peered past her reflection into the tidy dark: workbench clean, ledger closed, ribbon reels stacked by shade.

The baker from two doors down dried his hands and came over. "Frau West is punctual," he said, apology tucked into the words. "Every day. Today, nicht." He glanced toward the street. "Her bicycle isn't there."

They tried the landline; it rang inside the shop like a polite question with no one to answer. Hartmann called Carol's mobile—straight to voicemail. The landlord had no spare key. The rear alley gate was locked and tidy. No signs of forced entry, no reason for forced exit.

"Hospitals," Hartmann said. "Clinics. Any walk-ins overnight matching a knee abrasion." Dispatch came back clean. No Carol. No Jane Doe.

At Rathaus IT, the dome cam replayed Carol's return after the Nürnberg delivery. Nineteen fifty-eight—leaving the station road. 20:02—rolling past the bakery. 20:03—entering the wedge between two lamps where the plane tree turned light into lace. The camera surrendered her to glare and did not retrieve her. After 20:08, only ordinary walkers. No bicycle back past the lens before midnight.

Anja noted the gap, tight as a held breath. "We grid from the plane tree," she said. "CSU on the cobbles, rails, doorway seams."

Blue chalk returned to the cobbles like a memory. A CSU tech crouched with a headlamp that refused drama. He lifted a speck from between stones with micro-tweezers, the way a man picks a truth out of a rumour.

"Fiber," he said simply. Green, so fine it looked like light until it didn't.

Anja exhaled once. "Bag it."

She photographed the lamppost lines, the bench slat with the faint bell arc from two nights before, and the doorways' geometry.

"If it opened," the tech said, "it opened politely."

The street cleaner who'd once admired a woman scolding a "Riese" shook his head. "Heute früh, nichts." Nothing this morning.

A pensioner with a trolley said she'd passed at 20:10—the corner had been "schön ruhig." Beautifully quiet. The town had kept its word to be safe.

At Kripo, Hartmann drew a clean triangle on the board: last confirmed sighting, 18:30 at Nürnberg delivery; last local cam, 20:03, plane tree wedge. No return home. No shop open. No phone.

"Vermisstenfall—erwachsen, dringlicher Verdacht. Missing adult with urgent suspicion."

Not twenty-four hours, but urgency could be its own law.

Anja added a green dash next to the word Faser. "We treat the wedge as a scene. Canvass doorbells in fifty meters—quietly. Request doorbell cams, parked dashcams. Check railings for parallel scuffs. Flag anyone carrying green satin in the last forty-eight hours." She looked at the Orangerie note pinned from last night: Für den Klang.

Hartmann nodded. "And the club?"

"We have them on paper," Anja said. "No more today—unless a thread leads back."

The Call That Isn't n the evidence screen, Carol's mobile lit up with its last cell ping: 19:57, station road. After that, silence that felt too composed to be accident.

Anja stared at the blank where the next dot should have been and, for the first time that morning, allowed fear to take a chair. She capped her pen, squared the marker tray by reflex, and said, "We walk."

Outside, the church tested a single chime and decided it was not yet time to speak.

Chapter Thirty-One

The room had learned her breathing. That was new. Most rooms demanded people fit the space; this one adjusted by degrees, as if soundproofing had manners. Carol watched the square of light creep along the wall and decided to spend it carefully, like money.

"If this is a confession booth," she said, conversational, "I want the good kind of priest. The one who listens instead of grading."

"I don't grade," Vaughn answered from his square by the window. "I arrange."

"Then arrange this. My name is Carol Beverly West. I sell flowers because I like watching people lie about why they need them and then tell the truth anyway when the scent refuses to agree." She rolled her wrists once under the linen. "I don't like being tied. I can tolerate it if I understand the point."

"The point," he said, "is that you are here and not broken. And that I am not a rumour tonight."

"You're still a rumour. The kind that knocks people off bicycles and apologizes correctly." Her eyes flicked at the leather roll. "Sharp objects make terrible conversation starters."

He closed the roll with two fingers, slow enough to be language. "We can talk without props." He moved a chair opposite her, not looming, not shrinking, hands flat on his thighs as if placed deliberately neutral. "Tell me what you fear."

"Being made into a story I don't recognize." She nodded toward his ledger. "You keep lines. I keep petals. Neither of us likes mess. And you?"

He tried the wrong answer, discarded it, and gave her the true one. "Noise. People who confuse volume with truth. And losing count."

"Of bodies?" she asked. "Or of rules?"

"Of lines," he said. "The distance between things that keeps the world legible." His eyes touched her wrists. "If I free one hand, will you keep the lines?"

Her pulse kicked hard but she met it head on. "Terms. You tell me where the door is. I won't run yet. I don't like 'captive.' I prefer 'guest under protest.'"

He repeated it softly, as if shelving it in a glass case. "Guest under protest." He placed the ribbon halves parallel on the table. "The door is there. Neighbors. Courtyard cameras. If you run now, we both become someone else in their eyes. I don't want that yet."

He untied her right wrist with surgical precision. The marks were shallow, already fading. "Don't lie," he said, not threat but agreement.

"I won't. But I will ask unpleasant questions." She flexed and rubbed circulation back. "What do you do with quiet when you're alone?"

"I measure it."

"That's a job, not a life." She sipped awkwardly from the glass with one bound hand free. "Did you come looking for me?"

"No." A pause that sounded like truth. "Then I did."

"Because I organized you from a bench?" She smiled faintly. "You're welcome. Silence, sound, breath… I know the sequence. What comes after breath?"

"Choice," he said. The word fell like a coin on stone. "Sometimes mine. Sometimes not."

"Then choose a small truth. Your name. I won't use it unless you tell me to."

Silence balanced itself for a long beat. Then: "Vaughn." He let the name stand without falling. "You may keep calling me Riese if you prefer."

"Vaughn," she repeated, weighing it. "Good. It sounds like a man who irons his thoughts." She tilted her chin at the ledger. "You'll write this down later: 'Freed one hand. Subject did not run. Subject asked for name and returned it correctly.'"

A corner of his mouth moved, almost a smile. "Accurate."

Her eyes narrowed. "Another truth, then. I wasn't always a florist. I learned a different grammar before petals. Don't romanticize it. I don't."

"Then you recognize mine. The restraint. The measurements. It's easier to be precise than to be kind."

"You're proving that false right now." She lifted her still-bound wrist. "Kindness isn't taking me here. It's admitting what this is."

He didn't like speaking dirty truths into tidy rooms. He did it anyway. "You are here against your will. I took you because I wanted to keep a moment that should have ended. I don't intend to harm you without purpose. I don't yet know what purpose would look like."

Carol let the fear in—supervised, small. "Thank you for the sentence. Now a request. I want the other wrist back. Tie my ankle instead if you must."

"You negotiate like a professional."

"I sell roses to enemies and daisies to liars," she said. "Yes."

He untied the second wrist, no flourish. The marks were twins—parallel, shallow. He did not touch her ankle. Instead he moved the ribbon halves farther apart. "There," he said.

"Rule revision," she countered. "If I ask and you won't answer, say 'later.' Silence gets ideas."

"Later," he said, tasting the word she'd already called a name.

"Why lilies?"

"They insist on being what they are. No arrangement can change that."

"Then you picked the wrong woman. I'm the same."

She asked for the bathroom, then for paper. "To write a list," she explained. "What I will and won't do in exchange for not panicking. Also, groceries. Captives always get fed badly in books. I refuse to be under-seasoned."

"You prefer mint," he said without hesitation. "I remember the smell of your hands."

"Good," she said, smiling now by choice. "Then start with tea. And later you can tell me what you write when there's no body to justify the ink."

He looked at the ledger, at the ribbon halves, at the woman who refused every frame he tried. "Sometimes," he said, "I write the exact time a person made me listen."

Outside, a bicycle bell rang—someone else's, innocent and ordinary. The room absorbed it into the composition. Two green lines lay on the table, parallel and patient, waiting for whatever came after breath.

Chapter Thirty-Two

The kettle clicked off with the sound of agreement. Vaughn poured water into two thick glasses—no handles, no frills—and set them on the table with coasters that lined up like marching orders. Steam rose; the room condensed it into neat behaviour.

"Paper," Carol reminded him. "List time."

He produced a small notepad with squared pages and a pencil sharpened to a principled point. She wrote with her freed hand, awkward but legible:

Guest Under Protest – Terms

Water, bathroom, light. Ask/answer.

No shouting; no surprises with blades.

No lies; later beats silence.

I stay breathing; you keep doors honest.

Tea: mint if possible.

She slid the pad back. "Your turn."

He added his column with the same tidy cruelty he used on lines:

House Rules

A. No running; neighbors don't deserve that story.

B. Hands visible when asked.

C. If we leave this room, we leave as shadows.

D. If I say 'stop,' we stop.

E. I keep you intact.

"Define intact," she said.

"Alive," he answered. "Unmarked beyond what linen admits."

She nodded, not grateful so much as accounting. "Bathroom?"

He set an old brass timer on the table—three minutes, civilised. "Door closed. Window latched. If you need more time, ask."

She stood carefully, the room watching like a chaperone. In the small tiled space she took stock: a high window that opened a hand's width, thick glass; a bar of soap that smelled faintly of orange; a towel folded along a line so straight it could have been drawn. She washed her hands, pressed two damp fingertips to the tile beside the frame, and drew parallel lines no longer than a thumbnail. They would dry to nothing. She left them anyway.

Back at the table, she set the timer down with theatrical flourish. "See? Cooperative."

"Negotiator," he corrected softly.

He poured more hot water over the mint he had found in a paper packet. The scent reached the corners of the room and convinced them they were a garden.

"Question," she said. "Am I the first you've kept?"

His stillness seated itself. "Yes." A beat. "And the last, if I can count properly."

"Counting is your kink," she said lightly, and watched the word land without scandal.

The tea cooled to drinkable.

"Your turn," he said. "The 'other grammar' you learned."

"Later," she said, as promised, and sipped. "Your scar?" Her finger hovered in the air, not touching. "Lip line. Self or souvenir?"

"Both. I chose the second line by refusing to move." He did not elaborate.

Outside, a neighbor's footsteps and keys arranged themselves into proof that the world remained boring for most people. The sound moved on. The room kept their secret because that was the design.

"Why lilies?" she asked again, not because she'd forgotten the answer, but because repetition reveals cracks.

"Because they're honest," he said. "They won't pretend to be roses for anyone."

"Good," she said. "Honesty saves time." She set her glass down with a click that matched the kettle's earlier. "Do you intend to kill me?"

Silence behaved, then stepped aside. "No," he said. "Not while you keep making the hour make sense."

She breathed once, measuring the weight of it. "When do I see the door from the other side?"

"When the court holds. When I can walk you through the courtyard without changing into someone else."

She considered the math. Acceptance isn't surrender; it's a calendar. "Then give me work. Idle guests under protest steal cutlery. I'd rather arrange your shelves."

He almost smiled—a fraction that decided not to apologize for itself. "You can fix the window plants. They arrived in straight lines and forgot to be alive."

"So did you," she said, not cruelly. "Consider me hired."

He placed the notepad between them, open to blank squares. "Write what you need. Groceries, softer rope if you insist on knots, anything that keeps the lines and doesn't break the count."

She wrote: milk, bread, more mint, plasters (knee), lemons, string (cotton), and—after a pause—chalk.

He glanced at the last item. "For what?"

"To teach the room where to breathe. Chalk is kind because you can erase it."

He nodded as if the idea had a weight he could lift. The timer ticked without being needed, like a good boundary. He slid the glass toward her again.

"Drink first," he said. "Then the plants."

"And then?"

"Then you ask me about the ledger," he said. "And I decide how much ink is safe."

They drank mint tea and pretended the day was ordinary. The parallel green halves lay where she had told him to leave them—patient, exact, making a path they both pretended not to see.

Chapter Thirty-Three

The room carried mint in its corners, polite as a guest. Carol sat with wrists free, a concession disguised as trust, while Vaughn sharpened silence into shape.

"If you want something," she said, "you ask."

He considered. "Then I ask." His hand brushed her jaw, not command, not plea. "A kiss."

"Rule three," she reminded. "No surprises." But she leaned in anyway, her mouth pressing his with precision, brief and careful as punctuation. She broke first, eyes steady. "There. One sentence. Don't edit it."

The ledger on the sill waited like a witness. He didn't reach for it.

Later, bathroom again. The brass timer stood at three minutes. She smiled at it as if it were a conspirator and closed the door.

Window: high, narrow, German in its logic. She tested the latch, measured the swing, gauged the drop. Soap made her grip slick, towel dried it, chalk marks gave the wall a new memory: two short parallel lines, faint, erasable.

She used the towel for the sound—dropped it across the sill to soften her climb. Knees found brick, fingers mapped a grip. She lowered herself with controlled mess, breath caught, balance borrowed from the night.

The timer rang inside. She wasn't there to answer.

Vaughn entered. Linen folded on the chair. Glasses rinsed. Timer expired. Window unlatched. On the frame: faint chalk, twin lines. Parallel.

He touched them with two fingers, as if to check whether geometry could betray him. It hadn't. It had told the truth. No noise. No struggle. Only absence arranged as deliberately as presence.

Outside, the street belonged to ordinary sound: bakery trays clattering, a bell rehearsing Grüß Gott. Carol walked into it, head high, bicycle steadied, bruise aching but ignored. She passed witnesses and let them see her—let them mark that she existed in daylight, unbroken.

In the room, Vaughn sat with the ledger open and did not write. The word she had given him—Later—stayed at the edge of his mouth like a command he hadn't earned.

Chapter Thirty-Four

Carol kept her pace even. Running would advertise. Walking too slow would invite. She balanced between bakery windows and lamp posts, each step a negotiation between panic and stubbornness.

She entered the square with the calm of someone buying bread. A bell above a shop door chimed for another customer, proof that the town believed in its own safety. She let the sound wash over her like camouflage.

Carol checked the reflection in a bakery's glass. A tall figure remained at the edge, indistinct, a silhouette arranged by chance and choice. She lifted her chin. If she reached the threshold with witnesses, she would not be erased.

The bicycle bell gave one clean ding, unasked, as if the machine wanted to testify. A pensioner glanced up. A child tugged at her mother's hand. Eyes were turning; the moment had context now.

She reached the bakery door. "Police," she said simply, in German, loud enough for the shop to hear. Not a scream. A statement. The baker looked over, flour on his hands.

"Alles in Ordnung?" he asked. She nodded once. No collapse, no tears—just confirmation she was there, intact, being seen.

At headquarters, CSU laid out the wedge scene from the night before: fiber, chalk trace, window latch. No noise. Anja tapped the board where two green marks had been photographed from the sill. "She told the truth. Parallel, precise. She left us her grammar."

Hartmann folded his arms. "And he followed."

"Quiet pursuit," Anja said. "No panic. She created witnesses before he erased her. That's survival, not accident."

They logged bakery statements, CCTV angles, the dome cam's blind wedge. Each note tightened the triangle. Carol West: missing, then visible again, alive, confirmed. A survivor who insisted on being counted.

Chapter Thirty-Five

The brass dial finished speaking and the room did not give her back. Vaughn stood with one hand on the timer, feeling the metal cool the skin as if temperature could argue the moment into obedience. He did not call her name.

Names belong to rooms that consent to drama. The bathroom door opened on polite hinges. Window vertical, towel folded along the sill, mirror angled to mislead a first glance. Two chalk-pale marks on tile—parallel, short as a nail's breadth—pointed toward the open air with the grammar of permission denied.

Fury arrived the way winter does in a city that prides itself on order: quietly, everywhere at once. He did not throw anything. He put the towel back on its line, straightened the mirror, set the timer at zero. The mint in the glasses had softened to a green that forgave people for being poor at choices.

He walked the perimeter of the room the way a surveyor reclaims land after a flood. Linen coiled. Ribbon halves placed exactly where they had been left, not closer, not farther.

The ledger came to the table. He wrote in a hand that never hurried: 12:06 – timer – subject absent – exit: window (turn) – drop to courtyard – bicycle moved one meter. He stopped, and for the first time since he began keeping lines, the pencil left a mark he did not intend—an almost -curve before he corrected it into a straight.

He stood very still in the center of the floor and let fury be catalogued. It had edges. It had a weight that could be carried without breaking the lines—if he chose it. The choice wounded. That was new.

He acknowledged the wound like a craftsman acknowledges a nick: not fatal, not forgotten. She would go to witnesses. Bread, bells, people who practice Guten Tag like a pledge. She would borrow a room that already knew her name, say the word police, and the city would make space for her to be safe. He respected it. He despised it.

He kept breathing and allowed the room to resume being a room. The linen went into a cupboard where it would not look like evidence to anyone who didn't know the difference between order and ritual.

The ribbon halves stayed visible. A court would call it a spool. He called it a sentence fragment. He washed the glass she had used and dried it without noise. He washed the other glass and left a faint print on purpose—a right-hand whorl in a place any cleaner would touch later. Confession, decoy, both. He had not yet decided.

At the window he tilted the handle back to horizontal—tilt mode—and listened to the courtyard's squared air. No alarms. No hurried feet. Somewhere a child drew with chalk and the city allowed it.

He closed, latched, and returned the towel to a line he could live with. The question arrived and sat politely on the table: Will she bring the police? He answered it honestly. Yes. Not yet. Not here. She would change rooms before she changed roles. She would find witnesses first, words second, uniform third.

She was orderly even when improvising. He had chosen her partly for that. He opened the ledger again and added a single word he hadn't written before because it had never been true enough to deserve ink: Wunde. Wound. Then, beneath it, smaller: Kein Lärm. No noise.

He took the leather roll in both hands and felt what every

instrument maker feels when a tool is not the thing needed: weight without purpose. He put it back. He set a short length of green satin into the gutter of the book as a line he could close around later. Not now.

On the table, the kitchen timer waited like a pact. He set it again, without reason, to five minutes, and let it tick. Each click wrote a line inside his chest that felt like discipline pretending not to be grief.

He pictured the routes she would take: toward bread, toward people, toward a phone. He pictured uniforms in the square later, canvassing with softness, listening for a woman with a bicycle and a good face.

He pictured a knock that respected doors. He did not pretend it wouldn't come. He chose not to leave. If she brought the police, they would meet an apartment that had nothing to confess but order. A ledger with times but no nouns.

A man with clean hands and a bicycle bell that was not a trophy because he did not collect bells. He would be polite; he had practiced for years. Five minutes expired. He let them. He wrote the vow the way he wrote everything: without flourish.

Find subject. No composition. Quick.

It looked wrong in his hand, as if his letters refused to admit to haste. He underlined nothing. He closed the book and pressed his palm to its cover until the urge to put a second line beneath the first passed.

He sat. He listened to the small noises that prove a city is alive: pipes rehearsing, someone above moving a chair, a bird testing whether a courtyard can be owned. He waited long enough for choice to harden into plan.

Chapter Thirty-Six

Vaughn Aksel measured the café window like a lens. Glass reflected lamplight into angles, trimmed faces into fragments. Carol sat inside with two companions—posture formal, gestures tidy, not intimate but exact.

He could not hear the words, only the shapes of mouths, the tilt of heads, the rhythm of pauses. One of them—a man with a neat jaw, coat unbuttoned as if authority needed air—leaned forward. The other, a woman with hair pinned for efficiency, tapped a pen against a notebook. Carol listened, spoke, shook her head once, laughed once.

The laugh unsettled him. Too free for the hour. Too practiced to be mistake. He wrote it down in his mind: Subject laughs at him. Correction needed. From the street, her profile was half-lit, half-shadowed. She folded her hands on the table the way she tied ribbon—parallel, deliberate. She answered questions he could not hear, each word striking him as if it belonged to him.

He moved vantage to the arcade across the square. Through the glass, her lips framed syllables. He supplied the words himself: Riese. Bench. Bicycle. Kiss. Absence. His name—whether spoken or not—trembled at the edge of her mouth.

The man wrote something on a pad. The woman slid a document across. Carol signed. Vaughn's chest tightened. She was testifying. Writing him down in ink. Reducing him to evidence. A waiter placed cups, cleared plates. She touched the rim of a glass, traced a circle. He saw geometry everywhere. She was giving them his language.

When she rose, both companions stood with her, polite but protective. They walked in step, practiced. She belonged to them now. Vaughn followed at a measured distance, not near enough to be fact, not far enough to lose count.

They stopped at the church steps. Carol stood at the top, framed in stone, sunlight pressing her into visibility. She looked down at the square as if naming it hers. The man and woman flanked her. To anyone else, guardians. To Vaughn, thieves.

He whispered the word she had left him with: Später. Later. It fit his mouth like a vow. In his pocket, the ribbon edge warmed under his palm. He let the scene imprint itself: Carol in plain sight, allies at her side, the town believing her safe.

He closed the distance in his mind, not his body, and promised the ledger a new line when the hour allowed.

Chapter Thirty-Seven

Two mornings later the shop window bore a handwritten sign: Urlaub bis Montag. Holiday until Monday. The lettering was tidy, parallel strokes, no flourish.

Vaughn read it three times. The bicycle rack stood empty. Frau Klein watered the display daisies with dutiful hands, too steady to be invention. Customers asked, nodded, went on with their errands.

Holiday. Carol Beverly West had folded herself out of the square. The town accepted it with the same courtesy it gave closed bakeries. He did not. He walked the perimeter, found no bike, no fresh ribbons. He followed the rhythm of deliveries and learned nothing. Absence is also evidence.

At dusk he took a bus that left the old town believing in itself and entered countryside where hedgerows kept their own counsel. Colmberg's hill wore its castle like a ring; beyond it, a scatter of half-timbered houses practiced the art of existing without announcement.

He recognized the kind of rental a person chooses when they need a window and nothing else: second floor, square of light, line of ground he could count from the street. Mint in a box on the sill. Chalk marks too faint to bother anyone but a draftsman. He did not walk to the door. He walked past and past again, three different paces, three different coats in his mind.

On the fourth pass he found it: a small, deliberate imperfection—two lines in chalk at the bottom edge of a drainpipe, parallel and almost erased by honesty. It was her. Or it was someone who had learned to arrange a choice the way she had. He did not smile. Fury remained catalogued. The wound kept time. He turned the corner and came back in a way that made him part of the street's grammar.

The stair smelled of old wood and clean detergent. On the landing: a shoe rack that belonged to someone who liked to count—three pairs, heel-to-wall, toes aligned with the tile's grout. He raised a hand to knock and found the door already unlatched. Inside, a timer ticked with polite authority. The sound was both invitation and indictment.

He let the door rest against his palm and did not push it open yet. "Don't be stupid," he told his body in Norwegian, and then stepped into the room the way he had stepped into every room since he learned what rooms could do to men like him: slowly, with respect.

The apartment was smaller than his. Cleaner by design, not by fear. A kettle, cold. A ledger, closed. Two green satin halves on the table, set a fraction farther apart than he would have

allowed. On the windowsill, mint that had forgiven being transplanted. On the counter, a folded linen. On the chair, a scarf that remembered a shoulder without advertising it. He did not call her name. He did not say anything. He let the timer count down to the end of something and watched the numbers behave.

"You're late," Carol said from across the room.

No bravado. No tremor. Just the tone of a woman who had ordered a delivery and disliked delays. She wore black that belonged to work that wasn't floristry silent fabric, no shine and a cardigan that could be mistaken for warmth. Her hair was tied up; the shaved line at one side made order look like a decision rather than an accident.

She held no weapon he could see. That wasn't the same as unarmed. "I expected police," he said, because negotiations were more honest when they began with wrong guesses. "No police," she answered. "I've used them before. They come with noise." She stepped closer, enough to let her accent step with her—German shaped by Caribbean vowels that knew how to dance and how to cut.

"Sit, Riese."

Not a command. An invitation phrased as efficiency. He sat. He didn't like that he obeyed. He liked that he knew he did. She placed a glass in front of him, then one for herself. Water. Always water. She left the ledger closed between them like a bilingual text.

"We should talk about the thing you didn't put in your book," she said. "Me."

He considered standing and decided the geometry disagreed.

"Talk," he said.

"I was not born a florist," she said, and the sentence rearranged the air. "San Juan gave me a different curriculum. When I was nineteen, I worked for people who didn't put their names on invoices.

You would call it a cartel. We called it la familia. You'd know some of the men if you read the papers—Figueroa Agosto, the ones who ran money through islands and smiles." She didn't watch him for reaction. She watched the glass for meniscus. "I was useful because I was small, and kind when selling lilies, and cold when the work needed.

A clean line at the mouth—do you understand?—is not theater when you want people to fear an artist and not a butcher."

He understood too quickly and hated the speed of it. "You left," he said, aiming for flat and landing near respect. "I tried," she said. "Life is a ledger in that world. Debits follow you. Someone I loved paid a bill I racked up."

The only tremor in her voice was the one she let herself own. Then it was gone. "So I made a new grammar. Flowers. Mint. Chairs that face doors." The timer clicked to zero with the righteous finality of a rule obeyed. Neither of them moved.

"Why tell me?" he asked. "I am not a priest."

"Because you are a mirror," she said. "And you needed to see a version of yourself with different punctuation." She let that sit, then added, lightly, "Also because you're not the only one who knows how to track."

He did not look at the door. He looked at the places a person might have been—stairwell shadow, the building opposite with the lace curtain, the street where kindness congregated.

"Who?" he asked, though he already knew the answer was not a name.

"Old ghosts," she said. "People who owe me, people I owe. I left a trail they understand." She tapped the two chalk lines by the drainpipe outside with a finger in the air. "They taste like home from very far away."

"Are they here now?"

"Riese," she said with exasperated kindness, "if they were here now, we would not be speaking.

They are slower than you. They are slower than me." She leaned in, elbows on the table, chin tipped the way a woman tips it when she's about to save a man from himself. "But they will come. And when they do, the police will be a better noise than the one I left."

"You ask me to help you," he said, astonished to hear the idea choose his mouth.

"No," she said. "I ask you to decide what kind of silence you serve."

His mouth considered a slight twitch, then changed its mind, because the part of him that loved parallel lines recognized a rival religion.

"And if I choose wrong?"

"Then you make it quick," she said, and her voice didn't flinch. "Not because I fear pain. Because I refuse theater. If you're going to end a sentence, use a period, not confetti."

He looked at her and, finally—properly—allowed the thought he had been filing under later to write itself: she was not prey.

She was a hunter who had retired to a smaller forest and kept her knives in drawers labeled ribbon and tea. He could try to compose her. She would erase him.

"Why didn't you run farther?" he asked. "Because farther is louder," she said. "Here, I can borrow order. And because—" She stopped herself, smiled in a way that carried both San

Juan and Ansbach. "Because mint grows better in German windows."

In the hall, a footstep miscounted and corrected itself. Someone learned to carry groceries in a way that didn't bang the stair. Ordinary life cleared its throat and insisted on being counted.

"If I leave," he said, "I can keep you off your ghosts for a while. I can spoil their composition. I can write noise where they want silence."

"Good," she said. "Do that. And if you come back, you knock." A beat. "And you ask. No more taking. No more linen unless I agree to the knot."

He studied her face, framed by a window that refused to soften her. She didn't flinch. She didn't beg.

"Rule revision," he murmured. "Guest becomes host."

"Equals," she corrected. "Or nothing."

Silence arranged itself between them. He accepted it.

He stood. She didn't. He touched nothing on the table and let the ribbon halves stay the better distance she'd set.

At the door, he paused the way men do when they consider turning into a different person and decide they don't have time.

"One truth," he said. "You will not bring the police."

"No," she said. "But when the others arrive, I will choose the noise that saves the square."

He nodded. He stepped into the corridor and became architecture again.

Later, at the safehouse, he wrote: Urlaub — subject visible, subject declared grammar, subject not prey. He underlined once. Closed the book without sharpening the pencil.

Chapter Thirty-Eight

She lay awake later, mint cooling on her tongue, replaying the hinge where everything had tilted. Not the linen. Not even Vaughn. Before all that.

The bicycle, the rut in the cobbles, the shadow that steadied her—yes. But she hadn't told anyone what had truly broken her attention that night.

A Puerto Rican quarter, its face scarred with a pressed hibiscus flower in red enamel. She had found it on the ground near her shop, balanced on the stone like an offering. Hibiscus—the flower of San Juan, the sign she had promised herself she'd never see again.

She'd pocketed it without thought, mind gone elsewhere. That was when the wheel kissed the rut and gravity almost claimed her.

Later, when she carried lilies into Klang and Stille, she noticed the way certain eyes followed her—not as a florist, but as a ghost. Recognition without greeting. Her ribbons had betrayed her. Her face had not been forgotten.

Now, in the countryside house, with Vaughn standing where no one should, she felt it sharpening. He wasn't her past. He was present tense—dangerous—but he hadn't invented her ghosts. They had been waiting: patient, hibiscus-red, coin-bright, ledger open.

She wasn't running from Vaughn. Not entirely. She was running from the old grammar that had decided to speak her name again. He just happened to be an accidental addition to the grammar.

Interlude

Vaughn had lived his life in the still of early hours. Noise hushed by steel, and he did not blink. He moved through doorways and alleys like part of the architecture—stone, shadow, unremarked. His silence was perfect.

Until her…

Carol rewrote his grammar. The one entry he could not file in the cold ledger. He could imagine her blood—he could imagine everything—but not the thought of it belonging to anyone but him.

With her, obedience came without bargain. She spoke, and he moved. She commanded, and he carried it out. For a man who had never bent, it should have felt like breaking. Instead, it felt like home. He told himself it was possession—she was his. But the sharper truth was this: he had become hers. Her will cut deeper than any blade.

He had always believed nothing could undo him. Now he knew better. If she were taken, if her life ended by another hand, it would be the wound he could not kill his way out of.

So he bound himself to her in the only way he knew: possession, violent devotion, the vow that her blood and her breath were his alone.

Chapter Thirty-Nine

They found the bodies in a truck stop lot outside Nürnberg, rain still slick on the tarmac. The halogen lamps burned weak halos against the dark, turning every drop of water into a shard of glass. Two men lay propped against the wheel arch of a freight rig, stripped of IDs, cut with surgical neatness.

The CSU bent over them with gloved hands, cameras whispering in the dark, each flash carving the scene into fragments. One officer muttered something about gang retaliation; another cursed softly at the precision of the cuts.

Anja Vogel pinched a fiber bag between her fingers, holding it like evidence could stain her. Apfelgrün satin, Charge 41-D. The same green ribbon that had tied Carol West's bouquets.

Hartmann's jaw tightened as he turned toward her. "It's him. Again." His voice didn't rise; it sank, like a weight settling in a well.

Carol, watching from the periphery, said nothing. She kept her coat closed and her hands buried in her pockets, as though merely being near the scene could expose her. But her eyes—the eyes Vaughn had once measured from the dark—took in the details the police would never recognize.

The angle of the cuts. The absence of hesitation. The tidy removal of what could have been a spectacle. These weren't trophies. These weren't for pleasure. These were obstacles—cleared.

She pressed her lips together. Vaughn's grammar was present, yes, but it carried a different cadence tonight. No flourish. No pause to admire his own symmetry. He had carved a space, not signed a sentence.

Hartmann barked at a uniform to cordon the lot, breaking her thought.

Carol turned away, retreating into shadow, where her expression could soften without risk of being seen.

Later, in a room where no one else entered, Vaughn sat at a table lit only by the small circle of a lamp. The ledger lay open before him, paper pale as skin. His pencil moved with a kind of reverence.

Not mine. Noise removed. For her.

He closed the book with a measured exhale. The sound was small, but in the silence it was final, like the snap of a lock.

Chapter Forty

The café window turned the morning into glass geometry, all squares and angles that framed Carol like a still-life. She sat with Anja Vogel, their voices low, steam rising from the teacups as if it, too, were listening.

Vaughn stood across the square, motionless among the flow of pedestrians, his stillness making him invisible. He didn't need to hear the words; he measured the pauses, the tilt of Carol's head, the small narrowing of Anja's eyes when a point cut too close.

Carol laughed once. Short. Unplanned. It cut through Vaughn like the snap of a wire. Not at Anja—at him. She must be laughing at him. The door opened. A man entered. Broad shoulders, Caribbean sun baked into his skin, posture too disciplined for a tourist. He scanned the room once, the way soldiers are trained: exits, faces, threat. His eyes landed on Carol and stayed.

Vaughn shifted, leaving the reflection behind. He followed the geometry of the street until his shadow ran parallel with the man's. When the stranger left the café, Vaughn was already waiting.

They passed through the narrow cut of an alley where neon signs flickered above locked shutters. No words. No prelude. Vaughn's hand moved, the blade a whisper. One motion. The man's surprise was silent, his knees folding before sound could catch up. Vaughn lowered him carefully, as if shelving a book.

He wiped the blade once on the man's jacket and walked away without looking back. By the time he returned to his post, Carol's cup was empty. She was gone. She never glanced toward the alley, never asked a question.

That night, Vaughn poured water into a glass. His hands steady—too steady, as though memory had lodged under his skin. Carol noticed. She didn't comment. Her silence was its own mark, and it told him she had seen enough.

Chapter Forty-One

Rain traced silver lines down Carol's window, each drop dragging the night lower. Vaughn stood in the garden shadows, unmoving, his outline blurred by the storm. He counted her breaths through the glass the way others might count time.

Inside, she lit the lamp. A steady glow. She crossed the room, straightened the vase on the table, smoothed the cloth. Every motion measured, deliberate. She walked to the window, lifted the latch, and turned away. No mistake. No absent gesture. A signal.

The rain catalogued his stillness. Water slid down his face, ran over the scar at his jaw, and vanished into his collar. He didn't enter. Not yet. He waited—obedient, watching.

From her chair, Carol poured herself a cup of tea. She set the cup down without drinking and spoke softly, not raising her head: "If you want, you knock."

The night gave no reply. Vaughn remained outside, a figure written in rain, learning the difference between invitation and command.

Chapter Forty-Two

Carol's hands froze on the stems. A florist doesn't hesitate at lowers—but her pulse betrayed her. The hibiscus wasn't ornament. It was memory: salt on her tongue, debts in ledgers, men who never forgave. She set the bouquet down untouched. Safer to ignore than to acknowledge.

Across the street, Vaughn saw the pause, half a breath too long. That was enough.

The delivery man left with his satchel half-empty, walking too fast. Caribbean vowels, clipped and nervous. A man carrying more than flowers. Vaughn followed. Through arcades, past the station, into a shuttered lane—one stroke, silent steel. The body folded neatly, as if returned to storage.

That evening, the bouquet held only lilies, white throats yawning at the ceiling. She understood. Vaughn had seen. Acted. Removed.

And because he hadn't brought her the flower, she knew the truth: he was protecting her, not claiming her.

Chapter Forty-Three

They sat opposite each other. No ropes, no pretense, no glass between them. Just a table, two chairs, and air that carried more weight than chains.

Carol's eyes stayed on him as she set her palms flat. Steady.

"I've seen that flower before," she said. Her tone was flat, businesslike, as if she were cataloguing stock. "It means a debt. A warning. A promise."

Vaughn didn't answer. He was a man built of silences, and he let the pause hang until even silence seemed to shift.

"It belonged to a life I left behind," she went on. "Rules. Ledgers. Consequences. Not lilies." She held his stare without flinching. "But I understand your grammar because I once wrote in it."

Vaughn touched the spine of the ledger lying near his hand. He didn't open it. His thumb rested on the cover, pressure exact, as if to keep its words locked inside.

"And now?" His voice was low, neither threat nor invitation.

"Now," Carol said, "I refuse the script. I sell roses to liars and daisies to enemies. That's the business. But I remember enough to recognize you."

The room measured itself in silence again. Vaughn's scar twitched faintly when he exhaled, the closest he came to a reaction.

Carol leaned forward, just enough to mark the space. "You don't frighten me because you're new," she said. Her tone sharpened, almost cutting. "You frighten me because you're familiar."

The words landed like a mark struck into metal—permanent, visible even when polished over. Vaughn didn't move, but in the ledger of his mind, something unspoken had been written.

Chapter Forty-Four

The detectives pressed her hard. Hartmann's voice was firm, steady, a wall of authority: "We need you on record. You're the only consistent witness." Carol sat across from him, posture calm, hands folded neatly in her lap. Her smile didn't touch her eyes.

"I sell flowers," she said. "That's all I saw."

Anja frowned, pen scratching across her notebook. "You were at each scene, Carol. Ribbons, bouquets—patterns you can't pretend not to notice."

"I notice what customers pay for," Carol replied. Her tone was polite, almost helpful, but each word slid like glass.

"Roses, lilies, daisies. People buy what they want. That's all it means."

Hartmann leaned forward. "You're wasting time. If you know more—"

Carol's smile thinned. "Detective, I know stems and soil. Everything else is your ledger, not mine."

The silence that followed was thick with Hartmann's irritation. Anja looked down, scribbled again, but even she knew the wall had been built. Carol had bought herself time.

Chapter Forty-Five

The house smelled of steel washed clean and mint. Two men had followed the hibiscus coin to her, and now they were ledger entries with no names.

That night, Vaughn knocked and she opened the door herself then stood aside, saying nothing. He stepped inside. His shirt bore a stain—faint, almost invisible in the light. His hands were clenched, though his face remained stone.

"You killed for me," she said. It wasn't a question.

He didn't answer. Silence was his confession.

Carol closed the door, walked toward him, and stopped close enough that the damp of his sleeve brushed her arm. She touched his wrist lightly, a signal, not comfort.

"Then you'll obey me."

The ledger in his mind fell quiet. For the first time, Vaughn bowed—not with his body, but with the absence of resistance. Someone else had written the line, and he accepted it.

She had not thanked him. Thanks was too small for what he had done. He had killed not for symmetry, not for grammar, but for her.

"Sit," she said.

He obeyed.

"Hands where I can see them."

He placed them flat on his thighs, palms open, precise. The same obedience he gave to his knives, now offered to her.

She crossed the room slowly, untangling a length of cotton cord from her pocket. Not satin, not ritual—ordinary string, clean, soft. She looped it loosely around his wrists, not binding, just laying.

"If you want out, pull," she said. "If you want in, stay."

He did not move.

"Good," she said, and kissed him.

It wasn't like before. No punctuation, no test. This was grammar rewritten—her pace, her tempo, her breath. He followed not as predator but as student, learning her rhythm with careful hunger.

She pulled back, eyes steady. "Earn the rest."

He leaned into her, asking. She let him taste the answer, guiding his mouth, his hands, his silence. Each movement passed through her permission. The cotton fell away on its own, but he didn't notice. He hadn't moved.

When she drew him down to her, it was with the authority of someone who knew exactly what she was allowing. His touch was slow, deliberate, reverent. Precision had become devotion.

"Not ritual," she whispered against his throat. "Connection."

He answered with his body, wordless, his control surrendered piece by piece. The ledger in his mind fell silent; there was only her, and the hour, and the shape of her beneath his hands.

When it ended, she lay back and studied him like a composition she had corrected. He watched her with the astonishment of someone who had discovered a new rule and found it beautiful. Vaughn closed his eyes, as if the line between love and surrender had finally revealed itself.

Chapter Forty-Six

Carol walked the square with a bouquet meant for the church twelve lilies, two bands of green, no bow. In the middle of the mint she hid something small and ordinary: a brown envelope sealed against water. She set it on a pew as if leaving an apology.

Anja found it after vespers because of course she did. No fingerprints; sanitized paper; inside, copies of rental agreements and delivery dockets for a storage unit on the edge of town. The logo was discreet; the hibiscus watermark on one invoice was not. A hand—no one's—had circled a line: After-hours deliveries. Cash only.

Reiter signed the warrant with the same neat firmness as last time. Hartmann led the quiet entry with an Ordnungsamt observer who looked like a librarian and moved like a metronome.

Inside the unit: crates stamped for cleaning supplies that had never seen a mop. Plastic-wrapped pistols, ledger books with half the names in code and the other half arrogant. A roll of green satin ribbon, nine millimetre, Charge 41-D, tucked in beside a box of coins red enamel with red hibiscus.

"Germany base," Anja said. "Not the head. A throat."

Two men tried to slip out a back door with the indifference of people who believed in luck. CSU logged them intact. A third ran. He didn't make it far. By dawn, the storage unit belonged to evidence bags and bar codes. The press would get "ongoing inquiry," nothing more.

Hartmann looked at the hibiscus coins and then at Anja.

"Anonymous tip?"

She folded the envelope back into itself. "A town that refuses gossip can still tell the truth."

On her way out, she left a single green thread on the latch by accident—or so the latch would swear.

Chapter Forty-Seven

The man who ran wasn't clever, merely early. Vaughn found him at the freight spur behind the unit, hands shaking as he tried for a car with plates borrowed from someone careful.

No words. Vaughn disliked dialogue when truth was obvious. He put the man down fast, quiet, no composition. A correction, not a scene.

He stood after, breathing evenly, and watched the steam off the rails write sentences in a language no one reads. He left the body where it could be found by procedure, not children. He wiped no blade because none had strayed.

In the square that evening, shop closed, Carol counted the buckets on her step and knew what he had done without asking.

He came to her door and did not knock. He stood with his knuckles close, measuring the force he had always used on other doors and finding it useless here.

From inside, her voice, unhurried: "If you want, you knock."

He lowered his hand without touching wood. "Later," he said to no one, and meant it.

Chapter Forty-Eight

The press conference tasted of careful water. Reiter offered nouns that didn't bruise—arrests, seizures, cooperation. Hibiscus did not travel past the microphones. Neither did West's Florals.

Back upstairs, Anja ticked boxes that wouldn't stay ticked. "We've severed the local branch," she said. "The root is warmer. Overseas." Hartmann grunted agreement and underlined a word he didn't enjoy: copycat—the explanation they'd throw at any murder that didn't fit cleanly now that the hibiscus boxes existed. Vaughn remained the better suspect for the earlier women; the ribbon insisted.

In the late afternoon, Anja walked into Carol's shop and looked at mint as if it were a clue.

"We don't have to write your name anywhere," she said.

Carol tied cotton around stems, not meeting the detective's eyes. "It's just flowers," she said. The lie behaved itself.

Anja's gaze drifted to a reel of Apfelgrün set deeper on the shelf than usual. "Be careful," she said finally, which in German can mean I'm grateful or I see you or Don't make me choose later.

When she left, the bell announced her with good manners. Carol stood very still until the sound was gone.

Chapter Forty-Nine

Not loud. Not hurried. A measured touch that admitted it was asking permission from a door that owed him nothing.

She opened after a count that meant something to both of them. He stood with empty hands and a ledger under his arm, ribbon marking a page he hadn't had the courage to write.

"Rule," she said. "No knives in rooms where we breathe."

He turned his palms up. "None," he said.

She stepped aside. He entered the way a man enters a church that doesn't yet belong to him—quiet, eyes lowered without submission.

He set the ledger on her table and pushed it toward her. "I don't offer confessions," he said. "I offer record."

She did not open it. "I don't need your past."

"It contains my future," he said, and then, because she required truth stated plainly: "If you ask me to stop, I stop."

"In Germany," she said.

"Everywhere you stand," he answered.

She studied his face the way she studies stems—angle, line, what the light wants to do.

"You will not touch me without connection."

"I don't know how to do anything without you now," he said, and looked almost annoyed at his own accuracy.

She placed her hand at the center of his chest, where once she had poked a stranger from a bench and rearranged a life by accident.

"Then we finish this book without noise," she said. "And if there is a next, you will be invited."

He breathed. It sounded like surrender because it was.

Chapter Fifty

The parcel was small and unafraid of stamps. Carol slit it with a florist's knife and tipped its contents onto the counter: one coin enamelled with a red hibiscus; one photograph of a marina where the water had learned to be warm on purpose; one line in neat script: Miramar remembers. Family remembers more.

She held the coin between two fingers and let the past ring like a glass. The room didn't change. She had always preferred rooms that understood their job. Her phone chimed once. A single message from a number that existed only when it needed to: Later?

She set the coin on the table and laid a short length of cotton beside it, parallel. Then she wrote San Juan and added nothing else.

Across town, in a room with a timer that had learned patience, Vaughn looked at the word on his screen and didn't blink. He wrote in the ledger without sitting: Germany: closed. Noise controlled. Subject: alive, equal, in command. He marked the page with green ribbon, then replaced it with cotton.

At the river, the town rehearsed evening like a promise. Ducks owned the surface; bells counted without insisting. Carol locked her door, checked the window plants, and smiled at how straight she had taught them to be without dying for it.

When she stepped into the square, he was already in the shadow that fit him. He didn't move toward her until she tilted her head—yes, now—and then he did, unhurried, hands where she could see them.

They walked back to his place without speaking, which had become the truest kind of speech. Inside the light was dim, orange scent and mint filled the air.

"They won't stop," she said. "Marianna won't stop. Not until I go back. If I stay, this town suffers for me." Her voice was steady, not breaking. Her hands didn't tremble. What frightened her was not Marianna, not the men she would face in San Juan. What frightened her was herself—the machine she had buried beneath lilies and mint.

The machine that, once loosed, would bring noise instead of discipline. She knew how easy it would be to let go. How quickly she would thirst. She looked up at Vaughn, and for once she let him see something unarmored.

He mistook it for fragility. He could not read the truth: that her fear was not of dying, but of becoming who she had been trained to be.

"I go home," she said simply. "I pay what's owed."

"You don't go alone," he said.

She shook her head, almost smiling. "You don't understand. If I unravel, it won't be them that kills you. It'll be me."

He touched her face with hands that had only ever known discipline. "Then let me hold what you can't. Nothing gets past me."

She kissed him, not to thank, not to plead, but because tomorrow was not promised. Because she loved him, though she said nothing. The room was still, timer unwound, ledger closed.

When he entered her, it was not ritual. It was connection—slow, deep, tender. He moved as if each thrust could write a promise on her skin: that he would carry what she feared, that he would guard the hour even from herself. She let him, because for once she wanted to surrender her machine to someone else's control.

Her nails marked his back, not in violence but in proof. He whispered nothing, only pressed deeper, reassuring her in silence that she was not alone, that she was not lost.

When it ended, she lay against his chest, eyes open, listening to the drum inside him that still obeyed rhythm. He thought she was safe in his arms.

Epilogue — The Confession

Carol lay against Vaughn's chest, his arm heavy across her, breath deep with a discipline even in sleep. She watched him, studying the lines softened by rest, the scars that matched hers.

For the first time in years, she felt something she hadn't trusted herself to feel: safe.

Her fingers traced the cotton cord on the table, the parallel halves lit faintly by the lamp. She thought of San Juan—salt air, hibiscus coins, the ghosts that would not forgive. Tomorrow, the past would arrive with teeth.

Her throat tightened, not from fear of them, but of herself. He would never know that her greatest terror was her own appetite for blood.

She kissed his shoulder, lips lingering on skin too warm to belong to a killer. The words rose unbidden, small and sharp. "I love you."

His breath didn't change. He hadn't heard. She closed her eyes, letting the silence swallow the confession. She would not repeat it. She had given it once, and once was enough.

Then, slowly, she pulled open the drawer of her bedside table. Beneath folded linens lay a small keychain: no florist should own. From it dangled a single key, scratched and darkened. She turned it in her hand, thumb brushing the grooves, the shape that had once opened doors she swore she would never walk through again. Her secrets had never been buried under flowers. They had always been locked behind this key. She placed it around her neck.

Somewhere across the ocean, a single bunker light flickered to life. Armored vehicles rumbled awake, powerboats fueled in silence. The air itself seemed to brace itself.

"La Niña regresa. La sangre no perdona, papi."

The Girl is coming back. Blood doesn't forgive, man.

Printed in Dunstable, United Kingdom